Foreword

"Pastor" is a nice word. But I'm from the South, and we call 'em preachers.

I pray people will buy this book for their preachers and give it as a gift of healing, as a token of their apology for being so confoundedly awful and insufferable and nit-picking and judgmental and bizarre and pitiful and self-absorbed.

It is intended as a gift for seminary students who dream their impending careers will be miraculous gifts from God wherein they serve the elect with love, and their lives are uninterrupted scenes of brilliant preaching, tender-hearted pastoring, and light and lovely appreciation.

I am not bitter and cynical. The church is the body of Christ, and it operates as a font of light and love and joy and creation and freedom more often than it could if it were not the body of Christ. If the church were simply a misguided, deluded tangle of fighting, overgrown babies it would have gone out of existence 1900 years ago. Radio Bible teacher Steve Brown puts it even more succinctly. "If a business operated like the church, it would be broke in 30 days."

The church is my spiritual mother. My life springs from her. I am not writing as a former preacher embittered by my bad experiences, but rather as a working preacher who adores my folks (some more than others). I wrote this book not to make any of them feel bad, but rather to give us all a good laugh, a moment of renewal as we press on with our eyes on the prize.

But humor is always dangerous. I have done radio commentary, published newspaper columns, and spoken in public for more than 30 years. Jokes, wisecracks, smarting-off — all of this is fodder for misunderstanding. Feelings get hurt. Apologies have to be offered. Human relationships are messy enough to make some of us wish we had never heard of humor, especially humor that stands a chance of being misunderstood.

It's worth the risk. P. T. Barnum said he would rather entertain a nation than run it, and that reflects a mere smidgen of the good that can be done by those who make us laugh.

So, enjoy, but understand there is a risk. Know that I laugh most at myself, and when I find myself laughing more at others than myself, I always know it's time to make an adjustment.

Any similarity between the characters in this book and actual people is purely coincidental.

May the Lord bless you and keep you. Amen.

Acknowledgements

I owe lots of people my thanks. Charlie Milford (Charles the third) and Meg Barnhouse have been more indulgent that anybody should ask. My wife, Pam, and my children — Pepper, P. J., Jessie, Sarah, Katie, Heather, Vanessa, and Luke — have provided tremendous encouragement. My extended family (Mama, Daddy, Bill, Gloria, theirs, cousins, aunts, uncles) is a rock, especially Anita Wilkie who encouraged me to write instead of playing football in high school. For reasons only they will know, thank you to: Shirley Rawley, Earl Crow, Charlie Milford the second, Dewey Hobbs, Marian Benke, Barb Kimsey, Murphy Osborne (even Bill Osborne!!), Mary John Dye, Jeanne Ross Neal, Kim Taylor, Marti Haliburton, Gary Phillips, Gail Crider, Marianne Wise, Marie Fortune, Ellen Woodworth, Linda Whisnant, Carol K. Anthony, Beverly Foster, Yvonne Jones, Martha Birt, Dee Bowyer, Karen Kanes Floyd, Betsy Teter, John Lane, Gary Henderson, Ms. Burl, Thomas McBrayer Hicks, Sondra and Bernie Edwards, Jan Sailors, Judge Bob Orr, Joy Franklin, Elenora White, Thurman and Lenora Padgham, Sandy and Nancy Dameron, Penn and Vicki Dameron, Nancy and Joe Ogle, Larry Jenkins, Sandra Epperson, Grady Wacaster, Tronda Pendleton and Phil Sprinkle and the members and friends of Tanner's Grove United Methodist Church, Mt. Hebron United Methodist Church, First Baptist Church in Marion, Boone United Methodist Church, and all my glorious new friends at Smyth & Helwys, including but not limited to: David Cassady, Sherry Meeks, Kelley Land, Mark McElroy, Jim Burt, Barclay Burns, Vickie Frayne, and Keith Gammons.

"Blessed are you who
are persecuted for my name's sake."

–Jesus

December 25

Yesterday, we had the worst cussed Christmas program in the history of the church. Shepherds in bathrobes, angels who looked like unmade beds, at least one of whom was picking her nose, and music that sounded like a cheap radio drowning out singers who could not care less. At the center of it all was the Rev. Arnold Chister.

The Rev. Arnold Chister pastors the Treadwell Freewill Baptist Church here in Nebo, NC. He is married to the Rev. Elizabeth Chister, who pastors the Nebo United Methodist Church, and her being a preacher is giving us Freewill Baptists a fit.

December 26

My boy, Wilson, and those grandkids came by for their presents. Acted like two hours at Grandma's was gonna kill them. If it was like the old days, the preacher would put the fear of God in them.

December 27

Clean-up after the Christmas program went like a fire drill. It's a wonder they didn't destroy the place. You Know Who was oblivious.

December 28

His wife is also oblivious.

December 29

His children don't have sense enough to come in out of a shower of rain. He's got a 14-year-old boy, Robert Taylor, a four-year-old girl, Tabitha, and they even bring foster kids into their house. Is he a preacher or a dad gum social services agency?

December 30

I'm sure his mother is a nice enough person, but I've heard his daddy was bad to drink.

December 31

He's been here four years, and he has yet to offer a Watch Night service. We used to bring in the new year on our knees. Instead he travels Down East to see some friend of his, and what you bet they do to bring in the new year? I doubt it has anything to do with praying.

January 1

My new year's resolution is to keep Rev. Chister on his toes. If I always let him know when folks need a visit or a comforting word, he'll appreciate all my help. Or if he doesn't, he'll hear about it.

January 2

Already I have had an opportunity to call Rev. Chister about Sister Irene's ingrown toenail. For some reason he didn't seem that appreciative. Even if it is his day off, does he think Sister Irene gets a day off from her toe?

January 3

He needs a haircut. God bless him. I think he has a heart for the Lord, and I know people from his generation wore their hair a little longer, but I hope he knows he would look much nicer if he would just trim it up a little.

January 4

The prayer room walls were fine before he painted them. What's wrong with white? Isn't white one of the colors that people associate with holiness and purity? What was it he said about earth tones?

January 5

Sister Irene called to say that Chister's wife had preached on the wise men. Well, that should make it clear that women have no place in the pulpit. If the Lord had intended women to preach, he could have sent wise women along with the wise men to the manger. And there's nothing in the Bible about the shepherds being women or even the angels. Go back and read your Bible, sister. None of the angels' names in the Bible are women's names. Hey, look at the nativity scene there in the front room. See? Even Jesus' father is a man. Seems plain enough to me.

January 6

Sister Eunice said one of those black teenagers Rev. Chister's so excited about having at church was eye-balling one of the white girls. Help me, God.

January 7

Bubba came by today. I don't know why we call him Bubba. He doesn't drive a pick-up or throw beer cans out the window. He drives a van with his tools on it. He fixed my washing machine again. I asked him if he was going to church anywhere, and he smiled and told me no. I told him I was worried about him. He said he'd be okay. I do wish the preacher would go see him.

January 8

Rev. Chister mentioned it was Elvis' birthday. Elvis. You'd think he could come up with somebody better than that to talk about.

January 9

Nobody from the church has been by or called in weeks. It was nice they came Christmas caroling, but you'd think they'd be more interested in me. I wish we had an old-fashioned preacher who would inspire people to do right.

January 10

Irene said her toe is better. The preacher's wife is leading a mission team from her church to Honduras, gonna lay block for a health clinic. You'd think they'd be people right here at home we could help. He still hasn't gotten a hair cut.

January 11

My boy Wilson's drinking again. I just know it. He hasn't admitted it to me, but he's been avoiding church and Sunday School. I'd die if people knew it, but I do wish the preacher would go see him. If my husband, Basil, was living, he'd die over this.

January 12

The preacher wrecked his car again. He's done it about four times in his years here. We always take a love offering to help him cover his deductible. He even told us he fell asleep at the wheel after his great-aunt's funeral. Lord, help. He's always making fun of himself. I don't see the humor.

January 13

Irene has a cousin at his wife's church. Her cousin said one of their members had a heart attack yesterday, and that woman's down there in Honduras working with people who can't even speak English.

January 14

He plays the guitar and sings in church. He's not that good. Some of the others say he's awful, but I know one or two like his Hank Williams stuff. It beats me why.

January 15

Irene brought her granddaughter to the church house. She's a softball coach in one of the high schools Down East. Well, that should be enough said, but she doesn't have a boyfriend, just to make the point plain enough. Rev. Chister hugged her like she was a normal person, and then they grinned at each other. You'd think they were up to something.

January 16

He's got the deacon board to spend $300 on some family up in the holler, said social services was gonna take their foster kids if they didn't have a proper bathroom. Now what business is that of ours? The deacon board needs to start looking for a new preacher.

January 17

I need to pray. Lord, you know Wilson's drinking again. He didn't sound like himself again on the phone tonight. God, bless him. Give me some hope here, Lord. Let that preacher know how much we need a miracle. In Jesus' name. Amen.

January 18

His wife was at the church supper tonight. She needs to gain a few pounds. What is it with these modern women? She looks like that song from back in the sixties, "Skinny legs and all." She did get a nice tan in Honduras. That's probably what she went for.

January 19

More black folks are coming to church. Help me, Lord. If I'm wrong about this, show me somehow. Amen.

January 20

I walked the graveyard today and talked to Wilson's daddy. It's a beautiful old graveyard, but it looks mighty desolate in the winter.

I told him, Basil, did you ever think you'd see the day we'd have a preacher married to another preacher? Black folks in church with us? Lord only knows what all else?

Basil, I sure hope they've got rose-colored glasses in heaven.

January 21

Rev. Chister came by Wilson's tonight. I don't know what they talked about. I'd been begging him. He wanted Wilson to go to an AA meeting. Lord, let it be.

January 22

He's talking to the deacon board about taking our kids to Honduras next time.

January 23

His New Year's Eve buddy from Down East was here. They were talking about bilingual worship and bringing in the Mexicans. Only they weren't calling 'em Mexicans. Hispanolees or some such. That Down East boy is one of those modern preachers, too.

January 24

Irene's toe flared up again. No preacher visit. It's worse the second time. Not the toe, the lack of visits.

January 25

I told Eunice we may as well give up on him visiting much. He goes by the nursing home to see Iris Wells. He said Iris is a real inspiration to him, 92 years old, and up there in that nursing home with no feet. He said after one visit, she looked up at him and said, "The Lord bless you and keep you. The Lord hold you in the hollow of his hand." He'd have more stories if he visited more.

January 26

They live in the Methodist parsonage which is fair enough since we don't have one. He keeps a lot of his office hours there. Just doesn't seem right, a Baptist preacher's office in a Methodist building. Next thing you know she'll convert him to sprinkling.

January 27

I know a lot of people disagree with me, but if I was baptized by sprinkling by a Methodist woman preacher, I'd be scared it didn't count.

January 28

It snowed knee-deep to Wilt Chamberlain. Nobody's seen either one of them out shoveling the driveway. The kids have been out playing in the snow, but the grown-ups are nowhere to be seen. And both of them preachers.

January 29

It's melted a little. Eunice called to say nobody's called to check on her. It's just not like the old days. I checked on Irene, so I guess the three of us are checking on each other, like we could do anything if there was an emergency. A new preacher could come in here and get this mess organized.

January 30

He mentioned that Gandhi was killed on this date. He was in India years ago and said 800 million Indians stop whatever they are doing, park their cars, stop work in the fields, whatever they're doing, all 800 million of them to remember Gandhi on this date, to remember his changing the whole world with the force of his nonviolent love. Surely, the Rev. Mister Chister knows that Gandhi was not a Christian. Surely.

February 1

He's begging the church for van drivers again. Why do we need a van ministry? He's dragging the most rag-tag, ungodly looking teenagers in from the worst neighborhoods in the county. If they wanted to go to church, I'm sure there's one close enough for them to walk.

February 2

Bud Goforth volunteered to drive the van and to look for more van drivers. He called me. Well, I never. Then he said he was gonna call Wilson. Help me, Lord. Don't let Wilson drive those young'uns after he's been drinking.

February 3

Wilson said yes. If he gets killed, I'll never speak to him again.

February 4

He keeps preaching prayer. He keeps talking about how Jesus told us to stand forgiving when we pray. He tells us to search our hearts for anybody who has ever hurt us or made us angry or made us uncomfortable or…Lord, that man goes on and on. He says our prayers are more powerful if we forgive and release the pain of old hurts as we pray. Well, I certainly don't have anybody to forgive.

February 5

He's weaseled the money out of Homer Evans for another van. More rag-tag teenie boppers and less peace in the sanctuary are on their way. Lord, help us!

February 6

One of those rag-taggers got up in church and talked and made everybody cry. He said he'd tried to kill himself a couple of times, but that both of the Chisters and some of the youth ministry volunteers had really helped him, gotten him counseling at mental health, helped him set goals, helped him find a job and improve his school work. Goal setting! The boy needs the Gospel! Mental health! What is this world coming to? I'll talk to the deacon board soon enough.

February 7

I listened to Brother Willy Bob Willard from the Paradise Hope Garden in Santa Cruzo, California on the radio today. Now, there's a preacher!

February 8

Wilson missed driving the van for choir practice tonight. The Rev. Chistermeister had to drive. I had to call Wilson. He didn't want to talk, answered in grunts. If ol' Chissy Foot spent more time with my son and less time with rag taggers…

February 9

Rev. Willy Bob says the liberals are ruining mainline Christianity. You can bet your sweet potaters that the Rev. Mister Chister doesn't listen to the Rev. Willy Bob.

February 10

Eunice said she's tried forgiving people when she prays. She said she calls people to mind who have hurt her, says she even goes back thirty or forty years. She said she cried. You see? Now, he's got people crying in their own homes.

February 11

I tried forgiving people when I pray, but nobody came to mind. Oh, I do wish Mama had…but she's been dead ten years. Why dredge up the past? Oh, this preacher is not good for me.

February 12

You don't hear that preacher talk about Abraham Lincoln. Oh, no, he's more interested in Elvis and Gandhi.

February 13

Bubba came to church! Holy catfish. I hugged him like he was one of mine. Eunice said she called him after her crying fit the other day forgiving people. Somehow that did the trick with Bubba? Well, if people have to resort to mindless emotionalism, I have to wonder if it's worth it.

February 14

I miss Basil. I wish we had some kind of ministry for lonely widow women.

February 15

He got his hair cut. His nose is too big.

February 16

That boy of his, Robert Taylor they call him, is some kind of basketball star. Something else to distract him from serving the Lord's people.

February 17

Eunice will not give up on this forgiving prayer stuff! She said Arnold's got her praying as an intercessor for two of those rag-tags, said one of the girls got raped when she was little. Like we need that kind of information!

February 18

Frank and Ella Green joined the church. He's been in mental hospitals, jails, flop houses from here to New York City. Poor thing, she's short-order cooked all over the place to hold the family together. Of course, they're not going to contribute anything to the church. What is that man thinking? The deacon board has to seriously look at his goings on.

February 19

He got his car fixed. Thank God. It would have been terrible if he'd had to lead a funeral with the fender looking like that. Yes, we paid the deductible.

February 20

Bud Goforth called to check on me! Imagine that. I told him I was fine, which I guess I am, although I felt a lot better twenty years ago, but who didn't? We laughed about that. He said Wilson drove the van the other night for youth group. We're running two vans now and the rag tags are about to outnumber the rest of us at church.

February 21

The preacher is hiring one of those Christian rock bands. Look the other way, Basil, just look the other way!

February 22

He and his wife have four other churches going in on this rock band. They're gonna do a show at the high school. He's looking for enough bread and grape juice to do communion for the whole student body. Watch 'em, Lord. You know they'll sneak in something besides grape juice.

February 23

Irene said Eunice has lost her mind over this praying and forgiving people. Some women are coming from town out here and they've got a group going that's even got Episcopalians in it. I'm too tired to think about this.

February 24

Irene said she heard his wife preached against the death penalty. Now, there's one for you. Imagine what this country might come to without the death penalty. It's bad enough as it is.

February 25

The high school wants $500 for using the gym. He'll twist somebody's arm for the money. He says money should never stop us from doing God's will. A rock concert! Ha!

February 26

He got Wilson to an AA meeting! The Lord is good! If the Reverand worked like this all the time, I'd never complain.

February 27

He missed prayer meeting to watch his boy play basketball. They said the kid scored 18 points. I hope it was worth it. I'm calling the deacons.

February 28

Wilson sat in my kitchen with tears in his eyes. "Mama, I'm an alcoholic. I can't never drink again." I knelt by his chair and held him. We cried together. He told me, "I'm so sorry, Mama."

Then he told me he's gonna call Charlene. I think it's too soon. They've been divorced two years. I figured it was his drinking, but I never said anything. What could I say? He said Arnold doesn't think it's too soon.

Figures.

March 1

He took the day off. What? People are dying. My son has admitted for the first time in his life he's an alcoholic. David Brewster's cancer's gonna kill him pretty soon. Poor old Iris Wells is up there in that nursing home, and that preacher takes the day off. I bet his girl preacher wife did, too. I'll get Irene to call her cousin and find out.

March 2

Yep, she took the day off, too.

March 3

These prayer meetings are getting out of hand, moving from house to house. They're even going to the rag tags' houses, and the rag tags are starting to show up with their little brothers and sisters. Eunice can hardly talk about anything else. Irene and I are agreed they can do it without us.

March 4

I went with Wilson to an AA meeting. Lord, they do smoke some cigarettes. I couldn't stay.

March 5

Wilson found a smoke-free meeting. We had to drive halfway to Charlotte. There were more women at this one. Such horror stories I have never heard. One woman nearly killed her son in a car wreck. I cried with her. A bunch of us did. Is this the best way to deal with drinking?

March 6

A woman from town came to talk about building houses and renovating old houses for poor people. My Lord, what else does this wild man want us involved in?

March 7

Wilson called Charlene. Lord, I'm praying. Is she gonna want him back? Is it good? Is she somebody I need to forgive? I'm not even going there. I don't want to cry.

Too late.

March 8

You'd think after all we've been through, he'd have the good sense to know that Irene doesn't want a big fuss made just because she's having some tests run at the hospital. He prayed with her, which was nice enough, but such a fuss. The deacons have got to know there's somebody better out there.

March 9

Frank Green has not been back in church since he joined. Ella sits there like the queen of Sheba with those three children. She's a good woman, solid like a rock. You can bet Rev. Chister hasn't been to see Frank.

March 10

Nobody understood a word in this week's sermon.

March 11

Irene's got cancer. I sat with her and we cried and prayed and watched a little TV. We had pizza delivered. Her daughter, Angela, and her son-in-law, Scotty, came by. We cried some more. Her son-in-law ate most of the pizza. Arnold was at one of his son's basketball games.

March 12

Eunice says her group will pray for Irene which just drives me up the wall. They've got the private stock of God's power over at those new groups of theirs with their girl preachers and Episcopalians. Well, excuse me, but God knows Irene's hurting, and I don't think that crowd of fanatics is gonna get God any closer to figuring out some way to save Irene. Dear God, you just have to save her.

March 13

Jonquils are out. Chister needs to get Bubba over to mow the grass.

March 14

Robert Taylor's got a basketball tournament in Knoxville. The whole family's going for the whole weekend. That means some jackleg preacher in our pulpit. But maybe he'll be the one we're looking for, maybe better than the one we've got.

March 15

Irene's first treatment made her sick as a dog. I went over there. We cried. I took Chinese. I ate like a pig. She looked at her food and then over at me like killing wasn't good enough for me. I got the message, cleaned up the kitchen and went to the couch to see if there was anything on TV. Irene went to bed and slept some. I didn't go home, ended up spending the night.

March 16

Irene's got a pretty place. The sun comes up out her back windows. First thing in the morning, it's like the whole world is brand new.

The preacher's wife takes the kids to school. Guess he sleeps late.

I left before she woke up. I just couldn't face her. I'll be back. The answering machine was on at Wilson's. I hope that means he's at work and not just lying there listening to the phone ring. He's still going to meetings.

March 17

Irene didn't answer the phone. I went over, and she'd cried two boxes of Kleenex. Except for Angela and Scotty, who don't get by that much, her kids live in California and Texas. Her daughter Mary Beth's flying in, but that won't be for a few days, and she won't stay long. One sister's dead and the other one lives in Cleveland. I guess it'll be up to me and Eunice. You Know Who came by, but didn't stay long. He did pray a pretty prayer. Didn't mention forgiveness. Thank you, God.

March 18

Dreamed about Mama last night. I woke up crying. Irene must be getting to me. I wish Mama had kept Uncle Tipton away from me. God, I can't think about this.

The preacher's hair has grown back out. His big nose looks better, but that hair. Help me, Lord.

March 19

That rock concert's tomorrow night. They say it's selling out. Great, now he's gonna think he's some kind of Jesus.

Irene had a pretty good day. Bubba's still coming to church.

March 20

It sold out. The deacon board's never gonna fire him now. But I'm not giving up.

March 21

They danced. What can I say? I am not an old fuddy-duddy. Basil and I even went and shagged at Myrtle Beach a couple of times. There, I admitted it. But right here in McDowell County? At the high school? And they gave 'em all communion? Eunice's granddaughter called Eunice and went on and on about it. She says she gave her life to the Lord.

It'll take more than that, little sweetie.

Irene had a pretty good day.

March 22

I'm not telling this to make myself look good, but I cleaned Irene's house today. I believe I'll hire somebody next time. I don't clean my own house as well as I did hers. Eunice came by, but she didn't stay long. What kind of church have we turned into? Teenagers and race mixing. How can any good come of this?

March 23

Irene's second treatment. I feel like a giant has his hand around my chest squeezing. Dear God, where are you? And where is that preacher?

March 24

Irene's daughter, Mary Beth, stayed two days. Her husband's a lawyer in Houston. How nice for her. Maybe he could sue God for inflicting her mama. Don't even tell me anything about hidden sin. Irene Butterworth is as good a woman as God ever made. They cried. All three of us cried. That big-nosed preacher came by. He tried to joke around.

What a knucklehead. God have mercy on us all.

March 25

Wilson took Charlene out. I just can't believe it. Divorced two years, nearly two and a half. I know she's dated other men, and these days you know people don't just date, as if anybody needed to even mention such a thing. God, God, God, what are you thinking about? What is happening to my boy? What is this doing to his kids?

Billy and Jeanie. My heart floods with joy at those young'uns. I wouldn't take a truck load of gold for either one of them. I used to tell them that when they were little. Billy asked me one time, "Grandma, couldn't you take that gold and then use part of it to buy me back?"

That preacher should have told Wilson not to date Charlene so soon after getting sober.

March 26

Dreamed about Mama and Uncle Tipton again. The plumbing had broken all through the house. The three of us sat in the kitchen and water spurted out of everywhere. The fixtures, the walls, everywhere. I woke up in a puddle of my own tears.

Don't even be thinking I'm gonna talk to The Rev. Arnold Chister about this. Maybe Irene. Oh, Lord, no. She doesn't need anything else right now.

March 27

I think maybe Frank Green beats his wife. It's an awful thing to accuse somebody of, but she was a little stiff in church the other day. That jerk preacher had to mention domestic violence from the pulpit. You'd think he'd have more sense. Ella dropped her head into her hands, but only for a second. Her oldest boy, Allen, looked over at her. You'd think he'd have more sense.

March 28

Eunice has been talking to Irene about forgiveness. I could gleefully kill her and that preacher both. Don't tell me Irene needs to forgive somebody, and that's caused her to have cancer. I don't believe for a minute the Lord's that mean and ugly.

March 29

Well, if it's not obvious by now, that church is my life. I don't have anything else. But those rag tag teenagers and their little brothers and sisters are about to drive me to a fit. There's hardly any place to sit, and every fourth or fifth one is black. I didn't know there were that many black people in McDowell County! Deacons, come to your senses!

March 30

Now, Irene wants to talk about forgiveness. So I let her talk. Her Huntley's been dead for twenty years. She's actually a good bit older than me, but it feels like we've been friends forever. She said Huntley could be so hateful. Oh, I don't want to hear this. She said he would bad mouth her cooking and the way she kept house, and I had to admit he had a point there. Lord, I'm so sorry. She said it had helped to forgive him. I don't get it. Isn't he dead?

March 31

I walked through the graveyard on the way to Irene's today. Mostly I drive, but it does me good to get out and walk. I stopped at Basil's grave. He's got a pretty stone. Maybe we spent too much, but it has sure held up good for all these years. I stood there for a long time just looking and thinking about forgiveness.

I asked him, "You got anything you need forgiveness of?"

Nothing but silence.

April 1

I feel so whipped, not sure exactly what all I did before Irene got sick, but she's pretty much got my undivided attention now. She's still going on and on about "giving up the pain," and "releasing the hurt," she calls it. She says Eunice calls it, "letting the hurt drift away, opening our hearts to God's love and healing." Guess where she heard such tomfoolery?

April 2

Well, old madame "Let the pain float away" showed up on my doorstep. I held up my hand to let her know she was not getting me on this forgiveness bandwagon. Eunice said, "It's in the Bible." And I said, "So is animal sacrifice, but I'm not burning a bull in my backyard."

April 3

Spring training opened today. You never hear that preacher talk about baseball. All his stories are about football and basketball.

Irene got her wig. She looks good.

April 4

Okay, so he tells a baseball story every now and then. I love the one about Billy Sunday chasing a fly ball as fast as he could, and barely catching it in the edge of his glove. Reporters asked him what he was thinking. He said he wasn't thinking. He was praying. Well, what was he praying? "Lord, I need your help, and I need you to decide fast."

But mostly it's football and basketball.

April 5

I just got home from the hospital in Marion. Charlene and Wilson were in a wreck tonight coming home from a date. This is so hard to write. I think they'll both be fine, but they cracked ribs. Their faces were bruised. They looked awful. I held up good, brought the kids home with me, although they're teenagers.

I called the preacher's house. His wife said he was at some kind of training, and wouldn't be home until tomorrow. She offered to come over, but I told her, "no." She's a nice enough person, but no girl preacher is gonna pray over this Baptist. Well, I did let her say a little prayer, a very nice prayer, over the phone.

Wilson got a DUI.

April 6

Billy and Jeannie didn't have much to say on the way to school. We all said it looked like their parents were gonna live. Jeannie asked if she could stay home. I told her to go on to school. She nodded okay. Tough kid. She'll be better off not hanging around the hospital.

I stopped by Irene's and told her. It seems like all we do here lately is sob and wipe our noses. When I got to the hospital The Rev. Arnold Chister was there. He looked tired. He's doing too much. Another man was there. Arnold introduced him as Max something. Max is Wilson's sponsor in AA. I guess they mark this one up as a loss.

Wilson said he was sorry. Me too.

April 7

Another treatment for Irene. I drove her. The kids are back at their house. They rode the bus to school. Doctor's gonna let Mr. and Mrs. Evel Knievel out of the hospital today. I'm sorry. That was mean.

And of course, they aren't married. Not anymore.

April 8

Wilson wants me to help him pay for the lawyer on that DUI. He owes me more money than I'll ever count or see. Thank God, I've got good retirement from the phone company. I'd give more to the church if that preacher hadn't turned it into a teen center.

April 9

Charlene came by. She looked like the devil's nap sack.

"You think I'm the reason Wilson was drinking that night?" she asked me. I just turned and looked out the window.

"Well, I wasn't, and I'm not gonna take the blame. You never did like me, and you know it. How's a marriage supposed to stand a chance when a man has to chose between his wife and his mama?"

I didn't look back. She walked out. That was totally uncalled for.

The grass needs mowing at the church. The deacons need to either hire a new preacher or a goat.

April 10

The crybaby forgiveness club met at Irene's tonight. I did not go. I know I sound awful. I hate myself sometimes, but nothing is like it used to be. What is going on? People are talking about such personal things. Ella Green put Frank in jail last night for beating her. In jail, mind you. It just never would have happened twenty years ago. A woman would have gone to her mother's 'til things cooled off. And guess who sat with her in the magistrate's office while they filled out the warrant? Preacher girl. Am I the only one who sees the problem with this picture?

April 11

Irene said the crybaby forgiveness meeting was beautiful. I did not want to hear it. All this junk about healing. Irene needs healed of cancer, not her past hurts.

Charlene is over at Wilson's all the time now. If they want to get married again, Chister knows it will be the end for him. We Baptists do not marry divorced people, especially not drinking, wild-driving, crazy divorced people even if they did used to be married to each other.

April 12

Bubba wants to join the church. Rev. Chister says he'll baptize him in two weeks. That seems awfully fast to me, but glory to God if it's the real thing. We'll see.

April 13

Irene and I walked up the road a piece. She talked about being a little girl and playing with her dog. She said she loved that little dog so much and hated it getting hit by a car. I told her to shush. Chister drove by and waved. Can you imagine?

April 14

Lashon Davis is one of the rag tags. From that name I don't have to tell you he's a very good basketball player. A little joke there. He got up in church the other day and talked about staying out of trouble, staying out of jail, staying off drugs. My little alcoholic was right there in his pew saying, "Amen," and nodding. Charlene sat on one side, and I sat on the other.

The preacher beamed like he'd done it or something. You think everybody in that church doesn't know what Wilson did? He goes to court on the 25th. I have never been so ashamed in my life. I hope Basil's not watching from heaven.

April 15

I file my taxes in January. You Know Who's down at the post office licking stamps and collating copies. I just smiled when I saw him. The man will be late to his own funeral. And we're supposed to find all this charming. There's a last straw out there, and I'll find it.

April 16

Bubba came by and cleaned out my drains. Wilson could have done it, but he and Charlene are going to AA meetings again. I don't know who's checking the kids' homework.

I asked Bubba why he was joining the church. He looked at me kind of funny and pulled his britches up the way he always does.

"Rev. Chister says my sins are forgiven," he told me.

"What kind of sins you got, Bubba?" I asked him.

He scratched his chin and looked away, blew a big sigh, like maybe I had hurt his feelings or something.

"You don't wanna know, ma'am. You don't wanna know."

April 17

So he preached on forgiveness of sins, said that crowd at Palm Sunday was so tore up because they believed Jesus was gonna conquer the Romans, but they also loved him for forgiving sins. Said life was raw and hard back then, people dying right and left, nobody much made it to old age. The Romans lined the roads with anybody on a cross they took a notion to kill. He said people tasted death a lot more than we do today. I couldn't believe it with Irene sitting right there, and several widows besides me and Irene and Eunice in the church, and well, it just didn't seem to me he ought to have said that.

And what did that have to do with forgiving sins? He doesn't think any of us are scared of going to hell does he?

April 18

The Yankees beat the Red Sox in preseason. It won't be the last time. Basil used to joke that he loved Jesus Christ, the Democratic Party, and the New York Yankees, and he wasn't too sure in what order. Of course, that was a different Democratic Party back then.

Sometimes I worry the Rev. Arnold Chister might be a Democrat, probably an Atlanta Braves fan, too. He'd better watch his step. I have had it.

April 19

"Listen my children and you shall hear of the midnight ride of Paul Revere." I wonder if Paul Revere was as scared of the British as Irene and I are of this cancer?

Irene is a good friend. I don't know what's gonna happen. I guess she'll die. There I said it. And we'll say, "Death where is thy sting?" but she'll still be dead and gone and I'll miss her. And I know writing about it now won't be anything like living through losing her and missing her.

My anger is like poison in my gut. It burns and spreads and heats. Old age ain't for sissies, not that I'm that old, but I'm old enough to know it's not gonna get any easier. I'd just like to hit somebody.

I know Basil's better off and Irene will be soon enough, but this is not Alice stepping through the looking glass. No sir, not one bit.

April 20

He dresses out of thrift shops. Really. I'm not joking.

April 21

At the big Baptist church in Marion they have a series of Holy Week services. You don't hear much of a Freewill Baptist being asked to speak at one of those, but he was and he preached on the cleansing of the temple, the anger of Jesus because nobody saw the temple anymore as a house of prayer. The boy loves to talk about prayer. I wish he'd talk to the Lord about getting some of mine answered.

April 22

He's against the death penalty. That's it. The deacons won't put up with this I know.

April 23

Wilson and Charlene and the kids came by for lunch. We talked about hiding Easter eggs when they were little. Everybody laughed and had a good time. Charlene's not so bad.

April 24

The graveyard was covered with flowers. Some florist made out like a bandit, but it did look nice. Basil, do you like the graveyard all dolled up like that?

He preached on "Father forgive them for they know not what they do." The man is a broken record, over and over and over again. Forgive. Let it go. Open your hearts to the scar tissue that is holding you back from the power and the presence of Jesus.

What is he talking about? Basil, do they have chocolate bunnies in heaven?

April 25

What an old fool I am. I read back over yesterday's entry. Chocolate bunnies in heaven? Have I lost my mind? I told Irene about it and she laughed like maybe I am an old fool. Okay, Irene, it's not that funny.

Wilson's court date. There I sat in my Sunday finest with every drug dealer and drunk driver in the county. I thought I'd never find a parking place. It was Wilson's first. I guess I'm surprised at that. He drank in high school. He's been in and out of jobs. He and Charlene busted up twice before they got married. He's poured half his life down the toilet. I still hold my head up, though. I know what good the boy's got in him.

And there was the spiritual leader of our flock looking like he'd just dressed himself at a yard sale. It was good of him to come, and I almost broke down as we prayed together in the hallway.

A lot of the drug dealers didn't have their preachers with them.

April 26

Wilson will serve ten Saturdays in the county slammer, plus required AA meetings. Max, his sponsor, was there, too. He was very contrite before his honor, which I thought was good of him. Charlene even dabbed a Kleenex at the corner of her eye, which looked sincere. Who knows? Five hundred dollars in restitution and fifty hours of community service. Maybe he can cut the grass at church.

April 27

Irene says there's no shame in a man admitting he has a problem and doing something about it. I told her he was in AA before he had his little crime spree. She laughed. I asked her what was so funny, but she knew I had said crime spree to make her laugh. I love to make her laugh. Still you have to wonder if AA couldn't be a little more effective if these drunks had the fear of God in them, too. I'm tired. I'm going to bed.

April 28

Lashon Davis called and wanted to know if he could do any yard work. I asked him if he needed money. He said, "No, ma'am," he was just looking for a way to serve the body of Christ. I do need some stuff hauled off from my garage, so I told him to come on by.

I wonder if You Know Who is trying to butter me up. Some of those other teenagers called Irene and Eunice. It's a conspiracy. Surely the deacons will see through him.

April 29

The Yankees beat Cleveland. Don't tell me God doesn't answer prayer.

April 30

Irene's seventh treatment. There'll be ten before it's over. I know a lot of people survive cancer. She's chipper and tough and grins a lot. She likes me to rub her feet. I'm not sure how she talked me into that. Lashon got Bubba to bring his van over and help with the garage. They did a great job.

I'm on the phone to the deacons pretty steady. It's time for a change.

May 1

Hooray! Hooray! The first of May.

I do love spring. I can spend my whole life moaning and groaning, or I can get out and walk and look at things and make the most of life.

Eunice says the crying and forgiving meetings just keep growing. There are about ten sets of them now, and people are going off to Charlotte and Atlanta to get more training in how to lead people to it. Gimme a break. It sounds like a cult to me.

May 2

I dreamed about Mama again last night. Okay, I'm picking up the pattern. Eunice talks to me about forgiving, and I dream about Mama. Duh. I am not stupid. Oh, I wish I hadn't written that. It reminds me of Nixon saying, "I am not a crook." Anyway, in the dream, Mama is driving. Me and Uncle Tipton are in the back seat, and I keep begging Mama to turn around and look. She won't, and when she finally does, she's not Mama. She's me. So, yes, I am losing my mind, but I'm not going to Eunice's meeting.

May 3

Irene says they do a lot of deep breathing. I did not bring it up. She says they breathe and they imagine the person they need to forgive standing right in front of them. She says it takes a long time. They breathe and relax and concentrate on the presence of Jesus, whatever that means, and they breathe and relax and concentrate some more. I'm quite certain I would go to sleep.

May 4

He and his wife are both preaching this stuff. And get this, they say people need to heal emotionally, financially, socially, spiritually, even sexually, as well as physically.

Basil, when you get a minute, drop me a note from up there in heaven with the angels, and let me know just what sexual healing is. Ha! Oh, I know, you're probably too busy playing softball.

May 5

Bud Goforth called to check on me. I said I was fine. I asked him why he was calling to check on me. He said Arnold's really pushing the deacons to do ministry. I asked him if calling to check on me was ministry. He said he thought it was. He asked me to pray as an intercessor for the whole church, and I'll admit I could do more of that. I asked him what he thought about the preacher being against the death penalty. He said he wished he'd stay out of politics. I said, "Well, praise God, I'm not the only one who noticed."

May 6

I called Homer Evans and asked him what he thought about this death penalty thing. He agreed with me and Bud. Now, we're getting somewhere.

May 7

I told Irene enough was enough. She looked at me like I'd been left out in the rain. She said I couldn't be serious about wanting Arnold fired over his preaching against the death penalty. I couldn't believe her, and she couldn't believe me. It was like we were on different planets. Finally I said, "Well, that's not all," but she started crying, and dear Lord, that hardly seems like a fair tactic. I couldn't tell her, but the death penalty is ordained of God to protect us from murderers and rapists.

May 8

We tried to talk about it again. There was nothing doing, but a couple more deacons called me. I believe I can get it to a vote. Maybe Irene's medication has her thinking a tad off-kilter.

May 9

Bubba came by the house and wanted to know why I was out to get Rev. Chister. Well, it's as plain as the nose on your face I said to Bubba, but he just shook his head. I said, Bubba, the death penalty is right there in the Bible, and he said, "So's animal sacrifice, but I'm not burning a bull in my backyard." That Eunice, how dare she tell on me like that? Lookee here, Bubba, I told him, the man's just too liberal.

The evidence is everywhere. He stared at the light fixture in my kitchen for the longest time, then finally said, "Arnold led me to the Lord."

May 10

Charlene's spending the night at the house, right there with the kids at home and every thing. The preacher will not say one word about it. I'm spending about an hour a day on the phone with the deacons. There's fifteen of them. We just need eight.

May 11

Billy called, my own grandson. "Grandma, don't try to hurt Preacher Chister. He's can't help it he's a little wacko."

I told him, "You don't understand, son. You're too young. We've got to have standards for our preachers."

He said, "Grandma, he's helped a lot of kids."

May 12

They met for 45 minutes. The deacons are all men, of course, like the Bible says. They didn't have the backbone to do it. Bud Goforth came by. I could hardly look at him. He tried to talk to me about it. I've never been so humiliated in my life.

May 13

I'm packing for a road trip. Irene blubbered and said "Don't be gone long." I assured her I would not, but I just can't hang around here now. Big nose won. I lost. It's time to put a few miles on my car.

May 14

I spent the first night in Atlanta. The Omni Hotel looks like a space station in an Arthur C. Clarke novel. From the top balcony the inside of the hotel looks like a canyon. That's the way my insides feel. I did the right thing. It was something that had needed doing for a long time, and I lost.

May 15

The Daze Inn on the Interstate outside of Montgomery, Alabama, a town with a Martin Luther King Blvd. I guess Rev. Long Hair would love that. He has a picture of King hanging in his office. And in that picture, hanging on the wall of King's office? Gandhi.

May 16

New Orleans. My hotel's a short walk from Jackson Square. Cannons and churches. Grass and trees, but those are everywhere. Okay I've been praying. Four states from Eunice and Irene, I guess I can stand to admit I've never been much of one to pray. I mean, doesn't the Bible say the Lord already knows what we're going to pray for? But I'm too far from all I know. Except I do know God is real. He just has to be. So, God, here goes.

My name is Beverly Roberts. I am 70 years old. My husband and parents have been dead a long time, but I am healthy. I have good retirement from the phone company and have been drawing a nice social security check for eight years. My son is an alcoholic shacking up with his ex-wife. My grandchildren are probably smoking dope and looking at pornography on the internet. My heart feels like a brick. Will you help me? In Jesus name I pray. Amen.

May 17

Yes, I've called Irene every day. She feels fine. Only two more treatments. I'm crossing Texas. I was wrong. There are not trees everywhere. There was a Gideon Bible in my hotel room last night. I felt like such an old fool. I read 14 verses in the third chapter of First John. It said if you love, you know God, and if you don't, you don't know God. Guess who I thought of.

May 18

Still crossing Texas. How big is this thing? A salesman in a roadside diner started talking to me yesterday. Back home I would not have allowed it, but I am out of town. Besides, I'm an old woman. There's a little freedom in that. He wanted to talk about Jesus, and for some reason I'm keenly interested in that subject right now. He told me about hitchhiking as a young man, and praying to God for a ride and promising God he would witness if the Lord would send him a ride. Sure enough a car stopped right quick, and he started telling the Lord he wasn't sure this guy wanted to talk, the guy was real quiet, and well, you get the picture. He rode along with the guy the whole way and never did witness. When he got where they were going, he offered to give the guy some gas money. The guy looked at him and said, "Just get right with the Lord."

May 19

New Mexico, finally. Driving Texas is almost as bad as being pregnant. It just went on and on and on.

So I figure that guy in that diner was the answer to my prayer. The Lord wants me right with him. What does that mean, Lord? In Jesus' name I pray.

May 20

Did I mention I was driving to the Grand Canyon? Basil never wanted to drive it or fly out here. Said we couldn't afford it. We could afford a fishing boat. Don't go there. I stopped just a little ways out to call Eunice. Yes, Eunice. It's humiliating to admit. While the phone was ringing, I looked over at a big blue plastic cup of water I had set by the pay phone. The way the light reflected off the surface of the water inside the cup, it looked full. But it wasn't full. It was almost empty.

I got her answering machine.

May 21

Nearly a full day at the canyon. There just aren't words. The pictures do it no justice. Even flyovers in the movies. To stand here alone. To look out and be awe-stricken. You did this, God? How could I ever do anything for you?

May 22

Two days at the canyon. Got Eunice on the phone last night. I apologized for not ever coming to her crybaby forgiveness meetings. She laughed at that name. She said people come to meetings when they're ready, or books or prayers or counselors or whatever they need to take the next step toward God. I asked her how things were at church. She said people keep coming.

So I asked her if I were going to try her little forgiveness prayer stuff, maybe I would, maybe not, what would I need to do first? She said make a list of those people in my life who need to be forgiven. I thanked her and hung up the phone.

Mama and Uncle Tipton. My crybaby self went to it.

May 23

Day three at the Canyon. My motel is on the rim. I rise at dawn and go out without coffee or shower, just enough clothes to stay warm, and my God shows up like the Seventh Cavalry in some old Western. I've always thought God might be a little like John Wayne.

But these days he is everything. He is the water filling my blue plastic cup. He is sheets on the bed, wrapping me and holding me. He is the first light at dawn and the long shadows that cross the canyon. Eunice says let the hurt float away. I dump train loads of hurt into the Grand Canyon.

May 24

Irene wants me home. It took five days to get here, and this is day four here. I don't want to leave. But my home's in Nebo. Irene asked me last night on the phone, "Bev, something's happened hasn't it?" I hadn't told her anything. I told her I'd tell her when I got home.

I stood with a blanket around me, watched the sun come up one more time, and told the Grand Canyon goodbye.

May 25

Well, highs never last, and it took about three hours into New Mexico for the water pump to go out. The tow truck driver was a hairy, fat man who was not well turned out. I'm not sure how often they wash those coveralls, but today was not wash day. We rode along in the front of his tow truck. "You living for Jesus?" I asked him, and he just stared at me. "Got anybody you need to forgive?" I asked him. He stared a little harder.

May 26

Remembered that God had been in the sheets at my motel at the Canyon. Tried to get back to that feeling as I snuggled down in Taos. It wasn't there. I knew he was there, but feelings are funny. Spent the day walking around looking at people I don't know, buildings I don't know. I'm ready to go home.

May 27

Back in Texas. God, help me. Funny little phrase. I've used it as long as I can remember, but even it is different now. Maybe I believe that I mean it and that God hears it now. Oh, my goodness. I believe there's a commandment about using the name in vain. I know. I know. My sins are forgiven.

May 28

Texas.

May 29

Louisiana, crossed the Mississippi. Got out and kissed the ground. Not really, but imagined it. That'll do.

May 30

Mississippi and Alabama. Struck up a conversation with another old lady. You can bet your orange soda she wanted to talk about Jesus. Lord, was I ever like that?

June 1

And yes, I have stayed on the phone with Wilson. You think I'd drive to the Grand Canyon without telling my son where I was? He says he's still going to meetings. Charlene's gone with him. Been sober the whole time. Maybe I've been driving him to drink.

Uh.

You don't know how I wish I had not written that sentence.

June 2

Home. God, even this place looks different. You've changed me haven't you, old boy? I flipped through the mail and rushed to Irene's. You'd have thought Santa Claus came through her kitchen door. "Beverly!" she squealed like a school girl, and we nearly broke each other's ribs hugging. We talked for two hours and yes, I let her call Eunice, and that old bird about died when I told her about forgiving Mama and Uncle Tipton. I asked Irene if it was normal for a person to cry all day. She got the funniest look on her face, and said, "Bev, I've got bad news. You'll cry the rest of your life, but I've got good news. You'll laugh and sing and work and learn and celebrate the rest of your life, too. The hurts never stop hurting, but once you let them hurt, you can feel everything else too."

Yep, she's got it nailed. It's like feeling God in the sheets.

June 3

Old aggravation came by. God, if you really have changed my heart and made me a new creature in Christ, why do I still want to punch this preacher boy right in the nose? Old wineskins? What? You can't put my new spirit in this 70-year-old body? Oh, surely, that can't be it.

We talked about my experience. And yes, although I did not want to do it, I told him about Mama and Uncle Tipton. I told him what Uncle Tipton had done, not the details for goodness sake, but that it had happened, and that Mama didn't protect me. He was kind. He listened. You know how awful men can be about that, and he sighed and he prayed with me. Then he asked if I would be interested in talking with his wife about it. For some reason, I said yes.

Irene's last treatment.

June 4

She is a lovely woman. Too skinny, but lovely. Bird-like, perfectly proportioned features, nose, eyebrows, jaw line, chin. Elizabeth Chister, late 30's, early 40's maybe that's what I don't like about both of them. They are so young. I like being retired and not having to worry about money, having my house paid for and all that, but I'd love to have the strength I had at 30 or 20 or five, for goodness sake.

She listened. You gotta give points for that. It was just the two of us. I loved that I could tell the story without crying. She gave me a book about healing from sexual assault. Ugh. Wish they didn't have to call it that. I'll read it tomorrow.

June 5

One of the rag tags was arrested. He stole a car, went joy riding. His name is Charles. I care. This is a change. Thank you, Jesus. I even called the jail. They said I could see him. No, I said. Just tell him I called. They said they would.

June 6

Remember D-Day. So many died so fast. Hitler lost. Bad guys eventually always lose. I believe that. Another treatment for Irene. More meetings for Wilson and Charlene. Both my grandson and Arnold Chister's kids are playing ball. Baseball for the boys. Softball for the daughter. Holy catfish! I haven't watched the Yankees in three weeks. Oh, I was always afraid something like this would happen if I became a religious fanatic. There's a game on now!

June 7

All right! All right! I finally opened the cussed book. The ballgame was not that good. How amazing. I thought I was the only one something like this ever happened to. Sexual assault. There. I named it again. I think I'll go throw up now.

June 8

I drove over to the Nebo United Methodist Church. I'm pretty sure the Lord's not gonna strike me dead for walking in such a place, for sitting in the office of a girl preacher. Obviously, if you are reading this, I lived to tell it.

She was distracted. Somebody probably complained about the color of the paint in the prayer room. You know how people are. She let me talk some more, asked me what I thought of the book. I told her I threw up, then laughed, then she laughed. I didn't stay long. I could tell she was busy. Poor kid. I wonder what color she did paint that prayer room.

June 9

Charles is out of jail. I wonder what Rev. Chister's gonna do. No, wait. I'll call Charles.

June 10

I invited Charles over for ice cream. He said he didn't have a car. We both laughed. I asked if I could come get him. He said maybe some other time. He's gonna shoot hoops with his friends. "Okay, Charles. I'm praying for you, buddy." He said, "Thanks." Dumb little punk. He doesn't have a clue. Me neither, but lucky for me, I know I don't have a clue.

June 11

Billy's and Robert Taylor's baseball team won last night. I invited the Chister family and the Roberts family by my house for ice cream, and they came! I took a picture.

Charlene and Wilson, living like married people who are not, God have mercy; their two — Billy and Jeanie; and the preacher couple — Arnold and Elizabeth; and their two, Robert Taylor and that little Tabitha. It'll be a great picture. Tabitha said, "Miss Beverly, you sure do got good ice cream!" Yes, ma'am. I believe I do.

June 12

The cancer is not gone. I am. I am gone like somebody pulled my guts out. Eunice and I sat with her in her den. Magazines on the coffee table. The ceiling fan turned like they do in Casa Blanca. Everything else was still. It felt like three dead women waiting on somebody to find us and call the coroner. Finally, Irene spoke.

"They want to do radiation now."

I can't stand it. I can't stand it. God, you've taken me to the rim of the Grand Canyon and showed up like John Wayne on a horse, and now you want me to cry my eyes out watching Irene get her self burned to the ground by radiation treatment?

June 13

Eunice says we are going to research alternative treatments. Irene just looked at her. She carried a grocery bag full of books in from the library and the bookstore. Eunice spends money a little more liberally than I do. One of the books is by Larry Burkette. He got cancer a few years back and credits some kind of vitamin treatment in Europe for saving his life. How are we gonna get Irene to Europe? Of course, John Wayne can do anything.

June 14

Charles came by. Praise God! Oh, I can't believe I wrote that. I used to hate people who were always saying, "Praise God!" They always came across as so self-righteous and giddy. He ate some ice cream. This may be the ministry God is calling me to. Ice cream. He told me about stealing the car and how he and his mama always argue and how his daddy is in jail. I gave him a second helping of ice cream, and we prayed together. I'm still such a baby at praying. God, here's Charles and here's Beverly. We need you more than we need this here ice cream. Amen.

June 15

Irene has told her doctors, "No radiation." At least for now. Eunice has found a woman in Asheville who does what she calls healing touch. The elders have already laid on hands. I wonder if it's the same thing.

June 16

At the advice of that cussed book and my new friend, the girl preacher, I have written a letter to Uncle Tipton, which reads, "You knew you were wrong and you did it anyway. Did you think I would just grow up and forget about it? Well, in a way I did, you sorry piece of rotten snake meat. I didn't notice that maybe the memory of that pain might be hurting me when Basil and I wanted to make love. How's that make you feel, Old Uncle Stupid Slime Ball!!!!!" Me and my crybaby had a session. Then, in my mind, I walked to the rim of the Grand Canyon and opened my body like it had a velcro strip down the front and let the pain pour out like hot molten lava.

June 17

The healing touch woman is a sociology professor from Asheville named Kelly White, but this healing touch work she says has nothing to do with sociology. I'm glad she cleared that up. She wears her hair a little like Irene's granddaughter, the high school softball coach. I'll choose not to think about that. Eunice asked if it was okay for us to be there while she did her thing. She said it was fine with her if it was fine with Irene. Irene said sure. She stretched Irene out on the dinning room table like a corpse, something I didn't much care for, then started holding her shoulders, moved to her ankles, her knees, then just moved her hands in the air over Irene's body. I know, I couldn't believe it either. Irene cried like a baby. Eunice gave Kelly $50 and asked her to come back. What was that?

June 18

We met for lunch, took Irene out. Again, Eunice, you're spending too much money, but it's your money. This whole thing scares me. Is it black magic, voodoo, heebie jeebie? Eunice said it goes way back, not that different from the laying on of hands, but more Eastern, Chinese, Japanese.

Sounds fishy to me.

Irene said she could feel energy moving and emotions. Eunice asked her if it was like the work they do at their forgiveness meetings. Irene said, "Yes."

June 19

It's been two weeks since my trip, and I know everything that happened was real and powerful and ripped me out of the frames, but I still question it. Does that make sense? Have you ever had something really weird happen, and then you remember it and you remember that it did happen, but still you question it? I went back and read the entries from May 22 and 23, and I think, “That’s it?” Forgiving Mama and Uncle Tipton (the scum bag) and walking out to the rim of the Canyon and feeling God so powerful in everything? What does that mean? How do I explain that to people?

June 20

My first forgiveness meeting. You’d think Eunice would be smug to get me there, but she’s not. She’s a doll. I love her so much and my buddy, Irene. God, you are so good to give me these dear, dear friends. What would life be without them? Eunice opened with prayer. The place was packed. Eunice is doing two of these a week and six other group leaders are doing two to five per week. It’s like a cult. Just kidding. Elizabeth Chister is very active in it, leads one group in her church. It was about what you’d figure. Lots of talk about old hurts and new hurts and then the leader takes us through a time with our eyes closed where we let God and the angels and the river and the light and what all ever else take our pain away. Personally, I use the Grand Canyon.

June 21

The Rev. Arnold Chister preached on sin. Amazing. He says it’s an old Aramaic archery term which means missing the mark. You can bet it does, preacher boy. You can bet it does.

June 22

Yankees beat Detroit.

June 23

Kelly White came back and passed her hands around Irene. Irene says it feels like there are parts of her that literally are moved by all that hand passing. It's too woo woo for me. But wait a minute. God, please let this work. I don't care if it is woo woo. If it works, Lord Jesus, if I can keep my friend and not have to let her go, I don't care what it is.

June 24

They're running three vans now and have hired a guy, Sam Stimpson, to work full-time with the youth. Oh yes, I am giving more to the church. And yes, I called Bud Goforth and said I would drive the van. And yes, from the deepest place in my heart I pray, help me, God.

June 25

Halfway to Christmas. Maybe I can help with the play this year.

June 26

Took leave of my senses to have offered to drive the van. They are awful, constantly ragging on each other, whining, and moaning. Okay, so that's the bad news. The good news is that they have brilliant energy, like fireworks. I'll try to keep driving to a minimum. Nobody muttered anything about not liking an old lady. I was expecting worse.

June 27

Wilson's almost done with his Saturdays in jail, and no, I have not written about it. I cannot stand it. Oh, I need to be softer. God's a big bottle of fabric softener in my life. Jail has been too embarrassing to think about or write about, but that's my problem. Help me. I sound like those crybabies in the forgiveness group. Okay. Okay. They are not crybabies. I have cried, too. In fact, I am crying now.

June 28

So I've got to forgive Mama. I think I'd rather sit on a hot stove. But here goes. Mama, I forgive you for leaving Uncle Tipton alone with me. I forgive you for looking at me like I was crazy or speaking a foreign language when I tried to talk to you about it. I know, Mama, that you might be looking over my shoulder as I write, and I know you're in a better place now, a place where people don't cry. Right now, Mama, I wish you could cry. I'm letting it go, Mama, but there is just so much of it.

June 29

Yankees lost to Red Sox. What is this country coming to? Went to see Jeannie play softball tonight. Wow, that looks like fun. Maybe there's an old lady's league around here somewhere.

June 30

I walked three miles at sunset tonight. Eunice went with me. We made it out to Lake James and saw lots of boats and families having fun. It made me miss Basil.

Eunice encouraged me to talk. Of course, she would. That's what all this forgiveness stuff is about. I told her I had dreamed about Mama, talked to Mama, walked with Mama, that I felt Mama with us right there, right then. "And?" she asked me. It seems I am doing the work, and I may be doing the work for a long, long time. She smiled.

July 1

Kelly White came back and passed her hands over Irene. I've been there for all three of the sessions. Irene rolled into the fetal position. I'm not sure exactly how to put this but an energy came over the whole room. We were like in an earthquake, but nothing was shaking. The room didn't shake, it felt as though it was vibrating at a higher frequency. I closed my eyes and prayed. I felt God was there among us, but I know there are people who would say it was anything but God. Irene got up after about ten minutes, ten very long minutes, and said, "Let's go for a walk." We walked and talked like three women who had just been to a good movie. Irene looked wonderful.

July 2

My long-haired, big-nosed, goofy-driving preacher came by today. It was very awkward. I said, "Look, Reverand, we haven't really talked since the deacons met." He just sat there. I just sat there. "Beverly, I didn't come by to talk about that. I just came by to let you know I really appreciate your driving the van, to see how you're doing, and well…" — he stopped like he couldn't think quite how to say it — "to let you know I love you." Another long silence. Then, "That's mighty nice, Arnold."

July 3

He still bugs the fire out of me. I can't get a handle on it. It's like he can't do anything right, which he readily admits himself, and that bugs me, too. Be a man. Take a stand. Quit confessing how awful you are. It's unseemly. It makes you look like a fool. But then he quotes the Bible about our weakness being our strength, and God using foolishness in the world to shame the wise. Again, I pray most sincerely, God, help me.

July 4

Big fireworks over Lake James. I can't help but wonder if anybody remembers what it was all about. People died. People who could grow to be 70 years old like me, and have grandchildren and go for walks and eat ice cream, instead they got killed in that war.

July 5

Wilson's gonna marry Charlene again. I wish I had a nickel for every time I've prayed it would happen, but now that it's going to happen, I'm embarrassed. We don't marry divorced people in our denomination, and we don't ordain women. So the girl preacher is gonna do the ceremony, a double insult to our church. I know people think we're crazy and old fashioned, but we're just trying to live by the Bible.

July 6

They want a small wedding, and they want to do it in my backyard. I guess they want me to spring for the reception. Oh, I know that's cheap and unkind of me, but there you go. I'm feeling a little cheap and unkind today. Irene seems so much better. She sees her doctor tomorrow. Could she be healed?

July 7

I don't know what I think about miracles. I know they happen. Arnold Chister preaches on them every now and then. Says God answers prayer, but sometimes the answer is, "No." That's a little too cut and dried for me. The whole thing is a little hard for me to get my mind around. Does God want some people to die, die from cancer, die from car wrecks, die from wars, so that there's a grim and horrible backdrop against which miracles look really good, and he gets to look really good? Is the God I found so real and powerful at the Grand Canyon just a big show off? I don't think so.

July 8

They can't find any cancer. Irene is healed. They put her on one of those machines that make the clicks and clacks when they find the cancer. It purred in silence. Dear God, if it was you or Kelly White or the treatments or the combination thereof, thank you, thank you, thank you. I'm puddling up with joy.

July 9

Of course, I am going to let them have the wedding here in my backyard and yes, pay for the reception. I may be an old fuddy duddy, but I have my gracious moments.

July 10

I drove one of the vans for Vacation Bible School. We call it VBS. Those of us who have done it for fifty years call it VBS. It's like CIA and FBI. You don't have to say what it stands for. People just know. Have you ever stopped at a red light near a cattle truck and heard all the cows mooing? This van was much louder than that. Still, glory to God, some of them young'uns might be better off for the experience.

July 11

There are 267 children at VBS. About 40 something come by van. The rest of them get dropped off by their parents. Very few of us "stand in the gap," as the good book says, and do crafts, fix snacks, teach lessons, pray prayers, sing songs, and break up fights. I know this moment that I will have stars in my crown when I get to heaven. My back hurts. My feet hurt. I'm going to bed.

July 12

The state mental hospital is only 17 miles from my house. I know how to get there. I can drive myself, walk up to the main desk, tell them Franklin Roosevelt is president and I have come to bring peace from the Planet Zorak Four. They will lock me up and keep me until VBS is over. There were 289 of the little darlings tonight, and the Rev. Mister Chister wandered around like a lost puppy, grinning and hugging and telling them God loves them. Don't get me started.

July 13

Irene has been working VBS. Tonight even she was ready to machine gun the whole gaggle. But up until tonight, she had been a river of light. I guess I'd be beaming too if some miracle had snatched me from the jaws of death. We topped 300 tonight. It's over tomorrow. Thank you, Jesus. I've been thinking about Basil's pistol in the bedside table. Just kidding. All kidding comes from somewhere.

July 14

The parents show up for VBS graduation. They generally don't make eye contact. We serve hot dogs and tater chips. I think they think if they look at their hot dogs and tater chips instead of looking at us none of us will invite them back to church. Makes sense to me. But when their children are singing and moving their hands (never their feet, too close to dancing) and showing off the crafts they've made, you'd think these parents would bust with pride. I tend to swell up a might when my grandson hits a home run, too.

July 15

Help me, God. Nobody should have to write here what I do, but I cannot deal with this whole Chister thing without dealing with this. Ella Green is dead. God, God, God. I hardly knew her. I walked by her in church and spoke. That's it. That's all. I never called or went to see her when she had to put Frank in jail for beating her. I never asked if I could keep her kids any. Oh, God, I am swirling down my own drain. This is horrible. I want to say she was not my table to wait, but who was supposed to wait her table, bind her wounds, be her friend?

July 16

Frank has been charged with voluntary manslaughter. The DA says they fought. Frank claims she stabbed him. She fell against the edge of a table, no intent to kill. I may not have been Ella's friend, but I went over to see the kids tonight. They're all teenagers, two boys and a girl. They sat around like you'd figure they would. I had to admire them for holding up as well as they did. Arnold and Elizabeth Chister were both there. The girl, Sarah Jane, propped her head on Elizabeth's shoulder and stared into space. I took food which nobody touched, squeezed each one of them on the hand and hung around as long as I could stand it.

July 17

There is no time to trifle with life. It is simply too short.

Arnold was magnificent at the funeral. I never thought I'd live to write those words. He told us Ella is in heaven, and that she waits there joyously for a reunion with her children. He said if she could stand there with him at the front of the church she would bless her children to follow Jesus, to lay down their lives for the king of forgiveness, for the one who broke the chains of sin, and set us all free to walk as children of light. He talked about grief, how healthy it is no matter how badly we hurt, how sick and strange we would be if we did not hurt massively, hurt like fire, hurt until we thought we could not bear the hurt at the loss of Ella Green and at her going the way she went. I hugged him so tightly after that funeral. He still needs a haircut.

July 18

I went back to see the kids. Allen is 16, can live on his own in a year, which blows my mind. Keith is 15. Sarah Jane is 14. They're worried about having to live in foster homes, about having to be broken up. I drove home crying, so angry with God, something which Arnold told us was okay since the Psalmist had been angry with God, since even Jesus on the cross had quoted the Psalms, "Why hast thou forsaken me?" I called social services and told them I have three empty bedrooms. Basil and I had always figured we'd have more kids than just Wilson. The social services lady said she would have to do a home visit, but she'd like to come tomorrow. Tomorrow? God, you've pretty well figured this whole thing out, huh?

July 19

Hotter'n blazes. Air conditioning may be better than sliced bread. The social services lady was a doll, a little full-figured gal who grinned like sunshine on a cloudy day. I just wanted to take her home. She asked me about a thousand questions. Not really. It just felt that way. She wanted to know how I would feel about Frank visiting. I didn't hesitate. "He has to. He's their daddy. It may take them thirty years, but sooner or later they have to forgive him."

"Don't you think that's a lot to ask?" she asked me. All of a sudden my eyes turned to puddles. I told her, "It's a minimum requirement for graduation."

July 20

Irene wants to go swimming. She looks a little better than me in a bathing suit, but not much. The social worker talked to her supervisor and they will expedite a license to make me a foster parent. The kids' aunt, Frank's sister, came up from Florida. She looks like a train wreck. The bags under her eyes have bags. But she goes back to Florida in a couple of days. I've been over there every day. They all seem to appreciate me. I can't cook for pea turkey squat. But I know where the ice cream aisle is in the grocery store. They like ice cream. We took them swimming. All but the aunt, she stayed home and took a nap.

July 21

A fire inspection, a health inspection (I could whip that boy for looking in my cabinets,) and a criminal background check. And a check of my driving record. Boy, I hope they don't find that cocaine conviction. Just kidding. That cute little social worker came over and brought the gang. They look bigger somehow in my house. Wilson says I've lost my mind. He's right, but he's also jealous.

July 22

Irene went with me to Walmart. There's a band called "Southern Culture On The Skids." They've obviously seen some of my neighbors and their tattoos in the aisles at Walmart. I know the Lord made us all in his image, but sometimes he writes with an almost illegible hand.

July 23

That's it. They're here. After nearly 20 years out of the full-time motherhood business, I'm back in. Rev. Knucklehead came by to see my live-in rag tags. Keith and Allen each top six feet. Sarah Jane is a wisp of a pimply-faced model wanna be. Among them two gallons of milk per day is not enough. I'm looking to buy stock in a dairy. I walked with Rev. Chister out to his car. He shook his head. "Got any idea how long you signed up for?" he asked. I have prayed about this fiercely. My John Wayne God has been very clear about it. I told him, "Arnold, I expect all three of them to be standing around my deathbed." He prayed a very sweet prayer for me in the driveway.

July 24

They sleep a lot. Their mother was just murdered. Their father is in jail for the crime. There's no school. I'm not complaining. I walk with Irene every day we can. There is nothing spooky or weird or impractical about me. I change my oil every 3,000 miles. I read The McDowell News and The Reader's Digest. I would not be caught dead in a seance or a bingo game. I do not even believe in health food, so going to walk with a miracle cure every day is a bit much for me. She stopped today and asked me, "You don't believe it, do you?" I knew exactly what she meant, but could not bring myself to say it. "I was there. I saw it. I know you were cured." She then pointed out into a field by the side of the highway we walk past every day. I looked and Jesus was walking through the grass toward us. I told her, "I believe. Let's keep walking." Neither of us looked back.

July 25

Five months until my first Christmas as a foster mother. I'm redoing my budget. This is all Arnold Chister's fault. He's the one preaching all this justice for the poor, bringing all God's children in, breaking down the walls. I've heard people say they are more comfortable in a smaller church. Sometimes I think they mean they're more comfortable with a smaller heart. That was unkind. But I know it's so. It's where I was before I went to the Grand Canyon and found John Wayne.

July 26

Allen is what we call a big old Roebuck boy. He looks like he could wrestle a bear or fight a war. My Wilson is a more normal-sized man, and his daddy, Basil, was too, but this young Allen Green is big, dark-headed like his poor dead mama, and has the face of a man walking away from a car wreck. I hope to never see so much hurt on anybody's face ever again. It's a kind of permanent crumple. Maybe not permanent permanent, as in the rest of his life, but at least every day these days all day long. He sat in my kitchen this noon time, after just getting up. He was eating two peanut butter sandwiches and four cookies, with one of those fast food buckets they call a large cup filled with milk. He said, "You don't cook much, do you?"

July 27

The wedding is in three days. I can't get these kids to bring their laundry to the little nook in the kitchen where I do wash. Nor do they bring their plates and glasses out of their rooms. And they don't clean up after themselves if they fix anything to eat. I'm cutting them lots of slack because their daddy just killed their mama. It will not last much longer. I took Basil's pistol to Irene and told her under no circumstances to give it back to me. That is not a joke.

July 28

The wedding is day after tomorrow. No rehearsal. No attendants. Thank you, God. And no, that is not a throwaway expletive. That was a prayer. I'm very sensitive about this issue. Before Grand Canyon, I would God this and God that until I was blue in the face. It was not prayer. It was sin. I despise admitting that and admitting that I am ever tempted to sin anymore, but here I am playing Mother Teresa to three teenagers so, of course, under my breath, I sin about every three minutes. It's a good thing grace is sufficient to every need. Had it any outer limits, I believe I could find them.

July 29

We had a house meeting this noon. The wedding is tomorrow. I put a chore sheet on the refrigerator. I pointed to it as we talked. They wouldn't look at it. Keith is the quiet one, big as Allen, but red-headed like Frank. Nobody has made Frank's bail. Their furniture is in storage. I asked Keith, "Do you think you could bring your clothes to the washing machine, bring your dishes to the sink, and mop the kitchen once a week for starters? This won't be all. We've really got to work together to make this a home."

He paused a long time. He said, "You don't cook much, do you?"

We all laughed. I was so glad Irene has Basil's gun.

July 30

Wilson looked good. Max, his AA sponsor came to the wedding. I know nobody remembers this is the anniversary of Basil's death, eleven years ago now. That's okay. Elizabeth did a beautiful job, talking about second birth. Arnold came, looked ridiculous with his hair and thrift shop suit, but he was there. I could have kissed him. Not in the mouth. Billy and Jeanie kept eye-balling my new children. Sarah Jane stuck her tongue out at Jeanie while we were standing around eating peanuts and drinking punch after the ceremony. Irene and Eunice had helped me clean up and decorate. Everything looked real nice. Allen and Keith wore ties for only the second time in their lives. The first had been at their mama's funeral.

July 31

Well, Basil, did you see Charlene yesterday? She looked good didn't she, old buddy? I know about second birth now, Basil. I had one at the rim of the Grand Canyon. I'd love to take the whole world there, but you can't do it for somebody else, can you, Basil?

August 1

Sarah Jane wanted to go to the graveyard, so Irene and I took her. They don't yet have the marker there. Homer's gonna pay for it. He's seen as the money bags in our church, God bless him. Neither Irene nor I are exactly what you'd call fat, but next to this skinny kid we're like baby elephants. We stood in silence for a long time. It drove me pretty nutty, like maybe you could drive me any nuttier than I already am. I've cleaned up after drunks, gotten kinfolk out of jail, sat with Basil while he died from a leaky heart valve, but I never imagined standing with a teenaged prom queen wanna be after her daddy killed her mama. Is there some kind of Olympics for hard-luck stories?

August 2

Allen and Keith had not wanted to go the grave, but about eleven I strolled through and told Allen I didn't want to listen to the TV all night and have him sleep all day. I said, "Cut it off after what you're watching is over." He pretended not to hear me. I said it again. He didn't take his eyes off the electronic brain sucker, but he said just a little angrily, "I am sixteen years old." I sighed. I stood there like what felt like forever, maybe ten seconds. He didn't move. He's a very large boy. It probably takes a lot of energy to move him. I walked over, snapped off the boob tube, and spoke very slowly and very lowly, "You're in the biggest mess anybody around here ever dreamed of. I wouldn't trade places with you for all the gold in China and all the tea in Fort Knox, but life is what it is. School starts in a week. It's time to start sleeping at night and doing stuff during the day time. Good night, Allen." The other two kids were in their rooms reading, and I knew they were listening. I held my breath. His big sad eyes looked like a St. Bernard. He got up and went to bed. Thank you, Jesus.

August 3

The four of us worked together to mow my grass and Irene's. Ran both lawn mowers, the weed-eater, raked, pulled weeds, drank about a gallon of iced tea, and I felt horse whipped when it was over. Irene helped, too. Pizza and a movie was our reward. We agreed in advance to a romantic comedy. The boys would have preferred car crashes, but we couldn't risk anybody getting killed for entertainment. I'm sure our sensitivities will return to normal soon.

August 4

He said he wasn't going to bed last night. I said, "Yes. You are." He just ignored me. I lost it. I may be 70 years old, but I screamed bloody murder. Allen sat like a stonewall. Keith came in to watch. I told him to go back in his room and he did. Well, I didn't exactly tell. I screeched like a mortally wounded mythological creature, and he went back in his room. Allen kept sitting there. I ran about a half-gallon of water in a mop bucket and dumped it on his head. He shot out of his chair and hollered like he'd been shot, "What'd you do that for?" I hollered back, "It's a cure for deafness! Now, go to bed." He turned real red. He started to stick his finger in my face, but knew that wouldn't work. Stuttering and fighting back tears he said, "Even with pills, I don't sleep good." I melted and said, "I am so sorry." He asked to stay up a little longer, and I said okay. I told him he might want to sit in a different seat. He smiled and let me hug him good night. I went to the bathroom about four and he was still up staring at the television.

August 5

Me, Irene, and the kids did Eunice's yard today, sweated like pigs. I may be old and ugly but I know hard work reduces stress and these kids have enough to power a generator and light ten houses. Hey, wait a minute, there's something we can do with foster kids. All three are in bed. I just walked down the hall. They sound like they're sleeping.

August 6

Frank Green is a little wiry heathen. I know he's a baptized believer, but it didn't take. You don't live for the Lord and kill your children's mama. I don't care if they did rule it voluntary manslaughter. You beat a woman for years and one day slip and kill her? That's murder. I went with the kids. They said they wanted to see him. So we went. I know my own son has been in this same county jail, and I'm no better than anybody else, but still I'd like to do to him what he did to her. No. Wait a minute. I would not. I'm mad. I'm killing mad, but I don't have it in me. I couldn't kill the little wiry heathen, and I couldn't beat him for long, but I could sure dump a bucket of water on his head.

August 7

That cute little social worker, Kate Harris, said it was too soon for those kids to try to visit their cussed heathen daddy, and I agreed. They cried all the way home. Now, I am supposed to take them to forgiveness meetings and teach them how to let Jesus take all that pain away? Yeah, right, in about twenty years. I'd say they'll have to hurt pretty steady for at least that long. Shoot, I hurt over Uncle Tipton for about sixty-five years. I know. I know. The sooner the better.

August 8

I dropped them at the movies in Asheville tonight. Nobody knows them. At least, I hope not. I dread their going back to school. I pray the other kids are decent to them, but how in the name of all that's holy can they be? How can they not treat them like freaks? Anyway, Irene and

I went for ice cream and coffee. Sometimes I think I'm in love with her. Oh, get your mind out of the gutter. I just mean she is as dear to me as anybody living, and I hate she had to durn near die to show me. She looked tired. Shoot, we're all tired.

August 9

School starts in two days. I told them this morning we had to go shopping. They looked at each other and at me. "We want you to home school us, Aunt Beverly," Sarah Jane said. I just stood there. I did office work and public relations for the phone company before I retired. I've never taught, but I like books and obviously I like taking notes. We gathered around the kitchen table and talked. I called that cute little social worker, Kate Harris. She's coming over tomorrow.

August 10

You have to love Kate Harris, so much energy, such an easy laugh, so quick to tease and play and grin. I had told her on the phone about the home school idea, and she came prepared. "It's late," she said, "but not impossible. You guys are a special case. Everybody sees that. Nobody wants to embarrass you by forcing you into the center of attention at the high school. So, promise me you will stay active in church, keep doing yard work with Beverly and other folks at the church. Don't get isolated. Don't spend all your time in front of the TV, and I'll do the best I can." She nodded while she talked and made eye contact with all of us as she looked around my kitchen table. Everybody signed on.

August 11

I'm out of my league. No, not too old. No, not too stupid. There's something else. I certainly feel old and stupid a lot of the time, but that's not the problem with these kids. I know Paul said in Philippians that he, and by implication we, can do all things through Christ who strengthens us, but it is very hard to believe, very hard for me to see myself even as their foster mother. Now, after three weeks I'm supposed to be their home school teacher? I wonder, can they get extra credit for yard work?

August 12

We started with William Blake's "the road of excess leads to the palace of wisdom." They sat around my kitchen table. I have little books from the state, workbooks that have to be filled in, other books that have to be read, but I just threw out the Blake quote. What did they think it meant? Keith shrugged. I've got to cure him of that. It's too easy. I told him, "Keith, don't shrug. Think." But Sarah Jane beat him to it. "It means that even though our daddy did a horrible thing, if he'll learn from it, he'll be better for it."

August 13

Irene's helping. She is so amazing, and she was a school teacher. I watch her laughing and scolding and teasing and moving among those three kids. I adore her. They're all writing, but it's terrible writing. I help them rewrite. Keith, who almost never says anything, began his essay today with, "Sarah Jane don't love me. She said she wants to marry a man like Allen, not like Daddy. I'm gonna ask her what's the matter with me? I'd help her look for a nice tattooed, biker prince she could ride with. He'd be like me."

August 14

It's all about small victories. I remember loving Basil was like that. He drove me nuts the first few months I lived with him. He left his towels in the floor. I left the drawers open on the dresser. He rolled the toothpaste from the bottom of the tube. I squeezed from the middle. One day his mama caught me crying like a baby at the kitchen table. She came in and sat down and said, "Beverly, loving people is about letting them go. You don't let them go so they'll leave. You let them go so they can go and do and be. You put as much as you can into getting yourself right." I hadn't thought about that in years.

August 15

And it's about defeats. I think Allen is going crazy. He screamed in my face. "Leave me alone, old lady," was the nicest thing he screamed at the top of his lungs with the veins standing out on the sides of his neck. I wanted to call Kate Harris. I wanted to call the law. I wanted to call Irene to bring me Basil's pistol. Instead, I let him go. I went to my room and slammed the door. I think he thinks he won.

August 16

The day Elvis died. Arnold put that on the church calendar. Give me a break.

August 17

We need a road trip. I've had it with math, science, English, and geography. I'm taking the three amigos to The Grand Canyon. Their dad will be sentenced in a couple of days. I think I can get them to New Orleans in two days. If we take Irene's van, we can all ride pretty comfortably. Yes! She's going, too.

August 18

Not Atlanta. Six Flags Over Georgia. The difference between these two experiences is like the difference between parking a car and flying an airplane. They got me on that cussed roller coaster. I rode the log flume, the bumper cars, some kind of whirly-gig. I ate one too many hot dogs. The kids are in the pool. Irene's in the tub soaking out the soreness and drinking iced tea. Dear God, thank you for this moment of joy.

August 19

They don't like New Orleans as much. We haven't found the roller coaster. We did crack crab legs and suck down some gumbo on Bourbon Street tonight. Irene and I got Sarah Jane up to dance to a little Dixieland Jazz. Keith and Allen laughed their selves silly. I think Keith and Allen also provided protection for Sarah Jane, who got a good eye-balling from some of the lowlifes in the restaurant. Oh, all right, it was a bar. God, who has forgiven Jeffrey Dahmer and Ted Bundy, according to what I hear, will forgive Irene and me.

August 20

I called Arnold. They gave Frank 15 years. It makes me sick. It makes me want to stay in the bathroom a long, long time. I can feel the bile on my tongue. Arnold, of course, was not so upset. He even added, ever so nonchalantly, that he will serve max seven and a half, because North Carolina gives what they call "good time gain time," which is a day off for a day served. So this wife-beating, murdering wiry little heathen will be out the year his daughter turns 22. That's just not enough time. God, don't talk to me about forgiveness right now. Amen.

August 21

We're still driving across Texas. Took the kids to the Alamo. They yawned. I didn't even try to tell them. Irene was a little bored, too. How can anybody be bored with the place where Davy Crockett and Jim Bowie died? Oh God, death sure is a big part of life. Poor Ella. I know she's with you, now, Jesus, but she's with me, too. I feel her telling me how grateful she is that I have fallen in love with her big old children. Allen and Keith think they're men. Death, death, death. My mama, my poor daddy, who didn't have a clue about Uncle Tipton or Tip would have died a much younger man, Uncle Scuzball himself, and Basil, dear, dear, old bone-headed Basil, he was a good, good man, but of course he was a husband so I know everything that was wrong with him, too. Thank you, Jesus, for my dear departed ones. Keep me away from them as long as you can. Amen.

August 22

The kids love the Rockies. Having grown up with the Blue Ridge as a constant backdrop to their lives, they never imagined bigger, more rugged mountains. They're not too bad to travel with, more quiet than Wilson ever was on a trip. I buy them magazines at every stop. Keith, the number two boy, is crazy about motorcycles. God, help me. That was a prayer, not an aside. This is very important to me. Praying, not smarting off. As you can tell, smarting off is one of my worst sins. Arnold should preach more about sin.

August 23

I must be a genius to organize a road trip to New Mexico and Arizona in the heat of summer, but Irene's van is holding up well. Specifically, her air conditioner is holding up well. We've had it serviced today. A motel swimming pool is a godsend to two old women with teenagers. They swim, eat junk food, read their magazines, and leave us alone. I pray with them every day. I can tell it's a chore for them, but I think it is basic, basic, basic. Dear God, you have blessed us so deeply. Do with us what you will tomorrow, as we stand at the rim of the Grand Canyon.

August 24

Allen looked off the rim for five seconds then asked if we could ride the burrows into the canyon. What? No epiphany for my boy? No presence of the Holy Spirit sweeping in and making him cry like a baby? Five more seconds and Sarah Jane and Keith were right in there with him. "Please, please, Aunt Beverly. Can we ride the burrows into the canyon?" It's cheaper than the helicopter ride, I told Irene.

August 25

We're doing math and science and English and social studies and geography and all that other stuff as we travel. We have our little workbooks. Irene, glorious Irene, thought the canyon might be a good place to talk geology. The kids rolled their eyes, but they took it. We lassoed one of the park rangers to chat a little stratification. My, my, that girl was impressive. She told us the original architect on the canyon lodges was a woman, scandalized everybody wearing trousers and a Stetson hat. Now, you see that doesn't bother me as much as a girl preacher. Well, to be perfectly honest, girl preachers don't bother, bother, bother me. I'm down to about one bother. I still don't want to see some skirt in the pulpit.

August 26

Two more sunrises over the canyon, yesterday and today. Yes, it is different from last May. No, I am not enraptured as I was then. How does anybody get enraptured while keeping up with teenagers? But I still remember. Irene's gotten up with me. We talk a lot about the Bible. I know that sounds so goody two shoes, but it really isn't. This morning, she said to me, "Paul said we're supposed to rejoice in all things. It was hard during chemo. I'd be sicker than two dogs and wishing the Lord would take me home, but he wouldn't do it. So I would be hurting everywhere I knew to hurt. I'd wonder if anybody could rejoice in this. But I'd think of you and Eunice and my kids and I'd find a little something to rejoice in." I put my arm around her, and we snuggled our faces side by side and looked out at the dawn and the Grand Canyon. Sometimes it is not hard to rejoice in all things.

August 27

Heading home has turned at least one of my amigos back to his monster side. You guessed? Yes, Allen. He doesn't understand why we have to go back. Well, Aunt Beverly and Aunt Irene do have a pretty good incomes from their respective retirements, but not enough to support a permanent move to the canyon. Besides Nebo is home. "I'd like to never see Nebo again as long as I live," he snarled and growled and whined. Who can blame him? We told the kids the other night that their daddy would likely serve seven years for killing their mama. They said nothing. What could they say?

August 28

Six Flags over Texas gave us a reprieve. I feel like Allen's anger is an escape valve for the other two. But all three were happy enough to get back to roller coasters and twirly gigs. Irene and I soaked in the pool at the motel. I figure those big boys can keep the dogs away from their sister.

August 29

She wants to let her hair hang down into her face. Maybe she thinks zits will provide good cover. There are times when I think all men should be rounded up and shot. Just kidding. How hard would it be for them all to just act right?

August 30

Almost home. We're all tired of motels. Everybody got the day off from math and English and what all ever else is in those workbooks. But we did not take the day off from prayer. Precious God, who has swept into my life like John Wayne and the Seventh Cavalry, you tell those children you love them. I tell them. Irene tells them, we read in your Psalm 136 that your steadfast love endures forever. We read it 27 times. It's strange to me that after you said it 27 times so many of us still can't hear it.

August 31

Home. Eunice came over and hugged us all like we were just as precious as we could be. Arnold Chister called. Now, you see? He could have come over.

September 1

Charles called and talked to Sarah. Panic. Ultimate panic. This is what comes of mixing white children and black children in worship services. God, don't give me any lectures about love. This is a panic situation. This is a fear and trembling situation. You remember, God? We're supposed to work out our salvation in fear and trembling? I can't allow that black boy to date my white foster daughter. This is not negotiable, God. Don't mess with me on this one, Lord. In Jesus' name I pray. Amen.

September 2

Billy called and said Charlene and Wilson are fighting again. Oh, great, I've got to keep Charles away from Sarah

Jane, and I've got to pray up another miracle for Wilson. No, wait. Maybe this isn't all on my shoulders. What was it Basil's mama said about loving people is sometimes letting them go? Oh, God, how do I let Wilson go? Maybe if I faced the truth, he's been gone a long, long time. God, you help them. Amen.

September 3

Or maybe not. Wilson slept on my couch last night. It was a little tense because I had to explain to my big old Allen boy that if he didn't turn off the cussed television and go on to bed, Wilson would not be able to sleep on the couch. He towers over me. I look up into his face. He tried to negotiate, "Let him sleep in my bed. No more than I use it, the sheets can't be too dirty." That was true enough. But I held my ground. I put one foot behind me like I was bracing for a blow. Thank you, God, that Wilson didn't say a word. I think he was amazed at how his little old mama stood up to that big old teenager. Allen went on to bed.

September 4

Wilson told me in AA they teach one tactic for recovery called HALT, stopping whenever you get Hungry, Angry, Lonely, or Tired. He said it worked most of the time with him, but that Charlene just had a way of driving him nuts, little things, junk like Basil used to do to drive me nuts when we were first married. I explained what Basil's mama had said, you have to let people go. You can't fix people or change people or make them easier for you to get along with. You just have to let people be themselves. I think it maybe never occurred to him that Charlene driving him crazy was his problem instead of hers.

September 5

Wilson went home to Charlene. Charles came over to see Sarah Jane. I feel like there's a revolving door on my house. I told Sarah Jane before he got here that she could talk to him in the living room. "That's so old fashioned, Aunt Beverly," she whined, but I told her that she and Charles were too young for much time alone. I did not tell her that their being two different colors was an open invitation for the world to throw rocks at them. Eunice would say there might be some forgiving that needs doing around all this, but I say, black boys are just like white boys. They just want one thing. Only difference is, from what I hear, the black boys are a little more persuasive, and that's all Sarah Jane needs with her mama dead and her daddy in jail.

September 6

Hundreds of battered women are killed every year by their husbands, according to what our beloved pastor had to say in church. How come the boy can't use a little subtlety? My three amigos are sitting right there in the pew with me and Irene and he's spouting off about men killing their wives. We know it's wrong, preacher boy. We've cried a million tears over it. But we don't want it rubbed in our faces.

September 7

The Yankees have a lock on their division title. I wonder how I've lived without as much baseball as I have this summer? Did I imagine when my three amigos would come that they would blow me out of the ballpark? Where did I get the strength to go from living alone to living in teen central? Who would ever have dreamed it would cost so much? Could I have done it before I experienced God the way I did last May? And how can I have experienced God and yet remained so cussedly cranky and upset half the time?

September 8

Sarah Jane went with me to my forgiveness meeting. It still blows my mind. They tell us to take baby steps at first, and I had sure hoped S. J. would do that. Fat chance. She listened to Eunice talk about the principles, that so much of our lives remain stuck in the past, that so many of our problems from eating disorders to addictions often come from seeing our lives through layers and layers of pain, and often that pain comes from people we feel have wronged us in the past. Eunice talked about that hurt little child within us who vows at an early age to create a story better than the pain of that childhood. Eunice was just going on and on. I felt S. J.'s hand in mine and looked over at her. Tears streaked her face. Eunice asked, "Big hurt or little hurt, is there somebody you need to forgive today?" That little teenie bopper girl of mine sniffed and whispered to me, "Mama for staying with Daddy."

September 9

So we walked and talked about it. Irene and me and S. J. We walked out to Lake James State Park and watched the sun set over the mountains. We talked and talked and talked. I told her about my mama and Uncle Tipton. Old Tip was the heel's heel, but mama had let him get away with it. Somehow we think the bad guy is always the worst guy, but sometimes we hold more hate out for the good guy who wasn't good enough to stop him. Hitler was bad to the bone, but Roosevelt never allowed the allied bombers to hit the furnaces at Auschwitz. Little things like that are sometimes harder to forgive.

September 10

And S. J. wants to know if she has to forget. Is she to build her life on relationships of total trust, never wondering if another train wreck is in the cards somewhere? What can you say about people who survive train wrecks, house fires, dead dogs, cancer, prison? Does Jesus keep special closets full of crowns for the faithful who never stop believing even when they lose a hand in a press or accidentally back their cars over the neighbor's toddler? Oh, it's grim, but my babies will live with the memory of the night their mother died until the day each of them die, and if they ever have children, and in all likelihood they will, those children will live with the damage from that damage.

September 11

Charlene called to thank me. For what? She said Wilson is giving her more freedom than she ever dreamed. Apparently he took to heart our little chat about letting the poor girl be herself, about letting her go and do and be and celebrate life without having him breathe down her neck every second. That wasn't exactly how I had put it, but if it came out that way in her life, I'm thrilled. Jeannie got on the phone and said he's been an easier daddy to live with, too. Do tell.

September 12

Arnold wants us taking supper one night a month at the women's shelter. Have mercy, boy, don't we have enough to do. We're running four vans now, and to hear them talk in church, that youth pastor is doubling as social worker, motivational speaker, coach, shrink, and wet nurse. Okay, I exaggerate, but you get the picture. What else does he want us to do?

September 13

Math, science, social studies, English, geography, French, and now Allen wants to go to school, wants to play basketball. Help me. I called Kate Harris. She's on it, but Allen has talked to the basketball coach. He says it's a done deal. I told him, "Allen, you are white, and McDowell High is a 4A powerhouse, one of the biggest high schools in the state." He says it's a done deal. Suddenly my driveway is home to the thump, thump, thump of a basketball dribbling. Secretly, in the deepest secret place, I am thrilled. If he could make the team, even sitting on the bench would be better than sitting around here feeling sorry for himself.

September 14

We mowed grass, trimmed edges, ran the weed-eater, raked, hauled off brush for Bud Goforth. He paid us good. We had ice cream.

September 15

Thump, thump, thump, thump. Math, science, geography, social studies, English. What's the capital of Vermont? Main causes of The War Between the States? Theme of "The Taming of The Shrew?" S. J. says "No way," to "The Taming of The Shrew." Thump, thump, thump, thump. Tryouts are still a month away. Charles came over to see S. J. They were out of my sight for no more than five minutes at a time. She wanted to kill me. I only smiled.

September 16

Eunice and Bud Goforth's wife, Lucy, cooked supper at the women's shelter tonight. Am I supposed to feel guilty? I invited Charles' mother, Dana, over for supper. She works for the plastics plant in Marion. We had pizza. Allen explained, "We don't cook much." What a lovely boy. She and I walked out on the porch. I told Dana she's welcome at church. She looked at me a little sideways. "I didn't invite you over here to invite you to church," I told her. "Your son is spending a lot of time with my daughter, and I want you to know it's very important to me that they behave properly." Dana shook her head. "Who in the world can control a teenaged boy?" she asked. "Besides, she's not your daughter." I sighed. It's not easy. Nothing ever is. "I know you can't control him, but I wanted to get to know you, like maybe we could come across as being on the same team." She laughed. "It'll take more than one pizza. How about you come over to my house next time?"

September 17

Thump, thump, thump, thump. Arnold and Robert Taylor came by and shot some hoops with Allen. Now, there's a miracle. I asked the preacher if he knew the effects of the Dred Scott decision. He said he thought it meant slaves could be returned to their masters even from free states. I gave him a gold star and a cookie.

September 18

Chister says race keeps cooking our goose because we have never forgiven each other for the effects of slavery, the war, the Klan, the civil rights movement, race-baiting in political campaigns and the like. Oh, how these preachers do go on. Right now I am daily forgiving S. J. and Charles for liking each other so much. They watch TV and snuggle on the couch and kiss when they think I don't see. It turns my stomach, but it is my way of letting her go. Letting her get pregnant is something else. I know. If they want it badly enough, it happens. It happens all the time.

September 19

Arnold preached sexual purity. Was it enough?

September 20

Our culture is obsessed with sex, physical beauty, heat, lust, cha, cha, cha. I can tell you at 70, I sometimes feel a tad left out.

September 21

S. J. started her period today. Now, if she'll just do that for about the next ten years, I'll be so grateful. I'm sighing.

I'm praying. I'm not getting her birth control bills. Don't even start with me.

September 22

Thump, thump, thump, thump. The Chinese would not have needed water torture if they had just had basketballs and concrete driveways. No, wait. This is life. This boy is alive. He's got Keith out there with him. Wilson brings Billy over and even Jeannie and S. J. get in on the action. Thump on, big boy, thump on.

September 23

Kate says they will let him in school and give him credit for work done at home. She says she had to pull some strings, but one of the assistant principals went to bat for her and for Allen. Some people in this world are definitely for the kids. Thank you, God, for anybody who is for the kids, yes, even the Rev. Arnold Chister.

September 24

In the four years of Chister's preaching, six babies have been born in the church family out of wedlock. He says it is the greatest tribute to the pro-life politics of our congregation he can imagine. I'm so glad my dead mother never lived to see it. As bad as I hate to admit it, he's right. We hold baby showers just like these girls were married to the daddies of their babies. We dedicate the babies in the worship service, to the glory of God, that God might use them in some powerful and beautiful way to further his kingdom. That crazy preacher has even dared to say, "There are no bastards in God's kingdom," and I'll have to admit, you never hear that word in our church meeting house.

September 25

Dinner at Charles' house, with his mother, Dana, his brothers Tyrell and Simpson. It was a real meal. I couldn't help but think she was trying to show me up. My boys ate like hogs, and she had cooked roast, corn on the cob, creamed potatoes, green beans, sweet potato pie, and rolled-out biscuits. Maybe she knows my boys better than I do. We laughed like crazy. Especially when Keith maneuvered a huge cob of corn in one hand and a big spoon of potatoes dripping with gravy in the other. He grinned and looked at me, "This lady cooks much!" As the evening was ending, she pulled me aside. "How you think we're doing?" she asked. "God knows," I said and I meant it, but I like my new teammate.

September 26

We went back to prison. Frank's been moved to medium security down at Spindale. He'll be there for at least four years. If he earns minimum security, he might be able to attend his daughter's high school graduation. I doubt I'll home school forever. Allen's already back at the high school, and S. J. won't be far behind. My big old motorcycle man may be the last to go over. At 15 about all he can do is pick up cans on the side of the road to save for a motorcycle. My Lord, how can I stand by and watch him buy a motorcycle. I know. I know. Mama Roberts comes out of Ghost Town and whispers in my ear, "Let him go and do and be all that he can be." I don't think she's talking about joining the army.

September 27

Kelly White still visits Irene, and I am almost always there when she does. She still passes her hands over Irene's body and says she feels nothing out of the ordinary. Irene continues to talk about clearing anger, fear, hatefulness. Sometimes I think my hatefulness just grows two heads every time I cut one off. I'm glad anger is invisible for the most part. If all of mine suddenly sprang into sight, it might swallow up everything. Who am I still mad at? And why?

September 28

Charlene came over here squalling like a stuck pig. "He keeps bad-mouthing my cornbread." I told her, "You need to put another egg in it." You'd have thought I shot her. She screamed like she'd been run over by a car. "That's what he says," she sobbed.

I'm still learning this idea of letting people go. How do I let Charlene go and do and be all she can be when she's screaming bloody murder over putting another egg in her cornbread? Apparently both Wilson and I have a problem in this area.

Charlene heaved a little more, and sobbed, "It's not what he says. It's the way he says it." I think I know what she means.

September 29

Thump, thump, thump, thump, our boy may not be the greatest shot on the team, but he will know how to dribble. Several of the black kids in the church have come over and put him through some paces. I'm hardly subjective on this subject, but he looks like he's getting better. I have lavished the boy with encouragement.

September 30

They are all three in therapy, all three taking Prozac. This scares me a little. Although we did see a funny tee-shirt in the mall, "Give me Prozac and nobody gets hurt."

October 1

This whole trip has been so strange. Maybe I will never experience anything again like my trip to the canyon in May, but there is a little broadcast going on all the time, like God's got this low-frequency radio station, which keeps sending me word, "I love you, Beverly Roberts. You are absolutely fabulous." Well, that'll turn a girl's head every time.

October 2

Charles is over here nearly every day. It is exhausting. I know they are kissing, and young people who kiss usually want other stuff, too. Maybe they need a break from each other. How do I make that happen? God, you know everything. Give me some help here. How do I convince two jet engines to head for the hangers for a couple of weeks? They are obviously crazy about each other. I send him home by nine every night. S. J. is very unhappy with that, but she sulks rather than screaming. Maybe I could get Charlene to come over and give her screaming lessons.

October 3

Irene Butterworth is over here a lot. We play cards with S. J. and Charles. Mostly canasta. Kids these days think cards are so old fashioned, but they have a blast, especially when they make a good play. I feel such a sisterhood with Irene. It is deep and fierce. All this forgiving and praying and dumping anger into the Grand Canyon has given me more energy than I've felt in years. I feel alive, and I can tell Irene feels the same way. Sometimes I wish all these cussed kids would just go away. She reads and talks to me about books. She listens to the radio and asks me what I think about this idea or that idea. I'm teaching her to love the Yankees.

October 4

It goes without saying that the Yankees are in the series.

October 5

Black boy. White girl. Black boy. White girl. Thump, thump, thump, I feel like I'm spinning high in the air, watching myself from outside my body. Six months ago I was alone with my anger trapped deep in my heart, now I spin out of control, a top in the clouds over my little house in Nebo. Has God ordained before the foundations of the earth that Beverly Roberts would play referee for a teen romance, have her living room littered with biker magazines, her garage fill up with aluminum cans awaiting recyling and have her driveway fill up with basketball players? Or am I being bedeviled?

October 6

Irene's doctor said he wants to run a few tests. Nothing to be concerned about. The floor just came out from under me. We'll know in three days.

October 7

We'll know in two days. We knelt in the living room, buried our faces in the cushions of the couch and poured our hearts out like Pentecostals. All four kids — Allen, Keith, S. J., and Charles — prayed with us. I could have kissed them all, red and yellow, black and white, they are precious in his sight.

October 8

We'll know tomorrow. I said let's call Kelly, but Irene said wait. I'm afraid I already know.

October 9

The cancer is back. We all ended up at Irene's. Me, the kids (yes, all four), and Eunice and Arnold and Elizabeth Chister and other people from the church. I was immediately alarmed at the mob scene, but Irene seemed to flourish in the attention. "This is not to say that God doesn't answer prayer," she told us all at different times in the evening. "God's not done with me yet."

October 10

The Yankees won the series. Well, duh.

God, how come you can bring Joe Torre back from cancer? God, how come you can bring Lance Armstrong back from cancer? And then you turn around and give it back to my precious Irene? I know nobody lives forever. But this dear, dear friend of mine, God? Do you have to take her back into the hell of chemotherapy, back into sick, sick sickness?

I do love you with all my heart and all my mind and all my strength, but sometimes you confuse me and break my heart.

October 11

If I am tired, you will forgive me. If I am desperate, you will forgive me. If I yelled at all four kids tonight, you will forgive me. If I hid the basketball tonight, if only for a little while, you will forgive me.

October 12

Kelly White is back in our lives, passing her hands, asking the spirit, as she calls you, God, to come in and move her out of the way. Oh, God, oh, God, is that what it takes? Do you need me out of the way? Do you need me to just be a vessel for your spirit. I will do it, great God of glory. You just move me out of the way. You empty me of all that is not of you, and pour yourself through my hands, too, but do not let Irene Butterworth die, not now, not yet, ten more years, God. Fifteen.

October 13

David Brewster died back in the spring. I couldn't bear to write about it. Irene was taking chemo and I just couldn't write about it, but now, with her back in chemo, he comes to mind. He was an old man, yes ten years older than me, but he still died hard, fighting every step of the way. Dear God, I don't know how to die. Is it better to fight every step of the way? Or do we let go, let ourselves go the way you seem to be telling me to let other people go?

His brother took it the hardest. They said there were rarely two brothers who loved each other as much. His brother sat in the midst of the crowd at the funeral home with his face in his hands and cried like a baby. I think he's an old retired preacher. He's not from around here.

October 14

Irene wanted to take the kids up on Table Rock and look off at the gorge. They were gonna say no to her?

It is as beautiful as the canyon in a greener, smoother way. The hills are alive with light and color. I could stand there staring off for hours, but you know how kids are. We didn't get to stay nearly long enough. We held hands and prayed glory to God.

She starts her treatments tomorrow. I dread it like a toothache, but I'll be right there with her.

I didn't mention that night at her house, when we learned of this second bout, Arnold prayed the sweetest prayer.

October 15

She tries to buck up under the pain, but it takes her down like a wrestler. Body slam to the mat. She groans and I feel the meat twisting in my back. Charles and S. J. tried to watch TV in Irene's living room. I did not leave them alone at the house. S. J. has had another period.

October 16

"Aunt Beverly," S. J. said as she sat me down. "You can't watch us like a hawk forever. I like Charles and I like loving on him, but we're going to be good. You've got to trust me."

Yeah, right, I thought.

"I do trust you, dear. And I know you know you're too young for sex and babies."

"Yes, ma'am. I know," she said.

"What if Charles wants to move on?" I asked her.

She tipped her head to the side and dropped her jaw like that thought had never crossed her mind.

"Then he never loved me to start with," she said and smiled. "And God will help me find the boy who will love me." Ah, the faith of a child.

October 17

"The doctor says it is a more aggressive form of cancer," Irene said to me and Kelly. Kelly just sat there.

"Well, Sister Act, how about another miracle from your bag of tricks?" I fought back the crying in my voice and gestured at Kelly sort of the way Vanna White does prizes on TV.

“No bag. No tricks,” Kelly said and fought back a little crying of her own.

October 18

Thumper made it to tryouts today. He’s lost twenty pounds in a month and looks like a Greek god. So we need a miracle for Irene, but Allen’s transformation is proof enough for me that miracles really do happen. I wanted so badly to come watch, but the tryouts are closed. He said he did all right. Unfortunately in the South that can mean “mediocre” or “fantastic.”

October 19

Keith was in the lounger reading about motorcycles when Irene and I went out to walk. I told him I would bring back any cans I saw on the side of the road. He winked and gave me the thumbs up. S. J. and Charles were playing gin rummy at the kitchen table. I looked at both of them as we headed out. Irene held up very well, but we didn’t go far. We talked about the Bible. It says we are to rejoice in all things.

October 20

Allen Green will be among four white boys on the varsity basketball team at McDowell High this winter and spring. I know Jesus rose from the grave, but this has to rank among the top five or ten other miracles of history. His dad has phone privileges from prison. I handed the big guy the head set and watched a big tear streak each cheek. “Yeah, Daddy, they’re gonna let me play.”

October 21

The ground is littered with miracles. I sat on my back patio and looked at the leaves turning and looked at the grass and the rocks. Irene is a river of light. I cupped my right hand under her right elbow as she lay in her sick bed. I squeezed her elbow. She is sick, and she is in pain. I am not in denial about that.

October 22

My big boy Allen comes in from basketball practice very tired. He slumped into the rocker lounger tonight. Keith looked at him, and said, "Those niggers are gonna kill him." I groaned like I was gut shot. "How can that word just all of sudden appear in my home?" We all just looked at each other. "Okay, it's a totally wrong word," Allen said. "But he's right. They're killing me."

I think he thinks he has no chance of starting, maybe no chance of playing. Miracles, Jesus.

October 23

Wilson and Charlene are back fighting. Charlene asked girl preacher for counseling. Whoa! Praying and forgiving is one thing, but marriage counseling?

October 24

So, I hold Irene while she cries. We rock in each other arms. I fix halfway decent meals for the kids. I send Charles home by nine. My life revolves around other people. But I feel that John Wayne presence around me. I feel like that old song says, "He walks with me. He talks with me." Keith has about $200 in his can account. He can go work at flipping hamburgers when he turns sixteen. I'm afraid he's getting close to being able to buy some piece of junk motorcycle. Of course, I have no idea what they cost.

October 25

Keith was the last holdout to go back to school. He said it wasn't so bad. It gave me the school day with Irene. We held the forgiveness meeting at her house. Everybody laid hands on her and prayed. She smiled very sweetly and then said, "I do believe in miracles, but I also believe heaven is the ultimate miracle." I shook my head, closed my eyes, and blew out a long sigh through my nose.

October 26

Charlene and Wilson had a session with preacher girl. They came by the house afterward, and looked pretty rough. We sat in the living room because the kids were all in the den. "Charlene had a fling with Bubba while we were busted up." He looked at me like he expected me to fly off the handle and whip her right there on the spot. I sighed and shook my head just like I did yesterday listening to Irene talk about believing in miracles. "Do you love her, Wilson?" I asked him, but I know the answer. "You know I do, Mama." "Then see her with love's eyes and forgive her and let it go."

October 27

S. J. wants to be a witch for Halloween. I told her our church doesn't celebrate Halloween, although Arnold has been unenthusiastic about our alternative to Halloween, which we call, "The Great Pumpkin Witness." We don't celebrate witches and goblins and demons and such. S. J. says the witch of Endor in is the Bible. I looked it up. She's right. Something tells me they didn't wear pointed hats and ride brooms.

October 28

Allen wants to quit basketball. I just listened. Keith said, "I told you so." Allen looked at him. S. J. came into the kitchen. We were sitting around the table. "What's wrong?" she asked. Keith and I looked at Allen who looked at his little sister like she was an angel from heaven. "Are you gonna be at my first game?" he asked. She smirked and looked at us all like we'd lost our minds. "Of course."

October 29

We decided the witch of Endor could carry a wand with a star on the end. Anybody got any idea how to make a star stick to the end of a paper towel tube?

October 30

Group was good. Everybody asked about Irene. I hated all of them. They don't think of this as happening to them. This is happening to me.

October 31

Our goofy preacher did his heart-felt best tonight. He read from the Bible about the dead rising in Christ and reminded us of the ancient belief that the dead walk on November 1. Therefore we dress as ghosts and monsters to scare the dead away on Halloween, but he defended our tradition of not celebrating demons and witches and the old deceiver himself. My witch of Endor held her head high and threw a few spells hither and yon for good measure. Charles borrowed from Keith and decided a jacket and shades were costume enough.

November 1

Irene was sitting up in bed with her newspaper as always. I had brought doughnuts and started making coffee when she called for me to come into her room. She's hired a sitter, and she asked Mrs. Conley, the sitter, to leave so she could talk to me alone. Her beautiful old face had a tightness that gave it more lines. She's freckled and the wispy little bits of her hair that aren't white show how red it all once was.

"I'm dying, Beverly," she said ever so bravely, and I wanted to laugh in her face, but no, for once in my life I kept a straight face and didn't wisecrack my precious friend.

"I know, honey," I said as sweetly as I could and threw more arms open to hold her. She waved me to her and I held on while that high lonesome cry peeled out again.

November 2

McDowell tips off against East Burke in a week. His Aunt Irene will not likely have the strength to see Allen Green play. Poor kid. No mama, daddy's in jail, Aunt Beverly is a walking zombie trying to care for kids and her dying friend, and Aunt Irene is getting all the attention by being the dying friend.

She told the doctor, "no more treatments." He called Hospice. Call in the dogs. The hunt is over.

November 3

S. J. and Charles are taking care of Irene with me. They come home in the afternoons, do their homework, feed themselves from the vast variety of frozen pizzas and sandwich meats I keep in the house, and walk over to Irene's. She can sit in a chair long enough for me to change the sheets, and still gets to the bathroom on her own. But she is exhausted. I encourage the bedpan to give her a break. And yes, I change it. Arnold is here every third day or so. He prays a pretty prayer. The rest of us beg God for another miracle. He dares to pray, "Thy will be done." Who does he think he is?

November 4

Allen's seventeenth birthday. S. J. and Charles stayed with Irene so I could take him to dinner. He's not as tired after practice. I asked him how he likes it. "It's not what I thought it would be," he said. I asked for more. He told me how disciplined the team is, how tough the coaches are, how he has to think a lot more than he did in my driveway. He passed his test for his driver's license today. I told him we'd have to keep close tabs on each other, since we only have the one car. He said he'd like to drive down to Spindale tomorrow and take the kids to see their daddy.

As we were eating dessert, he looked over his hot fudge cake and asked me, "How you doing, Aunt Beverly?" I blinked back a few rivers of tears and squeezed his hand. "I'm thinking about becoming a Buddhist. You know they hit each other with boards to get tough enough for life's pain." He laughed, and I ate some more ice cream.

November 5

"Daddy's real proud of us," Keith, who almost never talks, said when they got back from the prison. Allen and Sarah nodded

November 6

The Hospice folks brought a jelly bean collection of pain killers, but it's not enough. She bends double and turns toward the wall. I get in the bed with her and hold her like a baby. Arnold, God bless him, came by and read from the Psalms tonight. Bud Goforth's been by to pray with us, and of course, Eunice is always here, every other day at least. And Kelly White comes and passes her hands over and cries with us and tells us angels are everywhere.

November 7

She's mad at God for not letting her just go on. We will have to talk when they call the roll up yonder. Of course, I want her just to stand up and walk out of the room.

November 8

Sometimes she sleeps and that is a grace. Mrs. Conley sleeps when Irene sleeps. So there I sit, usually with S. J. and Charles out in Irene's living room watching the electronic brain sucker. I watch Irene sleep. In ways, it is like being at the rim of the Grand Canyon. She is so beautiful and I love her so much. In sleep, she comes back to life, back from the pain, back to a hint of my old friend. And I thank God for her. And I thank God for being with us.

November 9

A preseason scrimmage against East Burke. The quality of play is awesome. These supple giants thunder up and down the court. It is like dance only noisier, like war without the blood. Do all these young men honestly believe they are NBA prospects, or do they just play this hard to win this one game?

Allen played a minute and a half, touched the ball twice, passed quickly after having it thrown to him. I told Irene she missed nothing. She winked and said, "I'm dying, Beverly. There are rainbows and waterfalls on the other side." Do tell.

November 10

She tells me she is not hallucinating, that she hallucinated once under a general anesthesia. "This is real," she told me in a voice fogged by drugs. "Angels come and go among waterfalls and rainbows. And the music, praise God, Beverly, the music is so beautiful, so hard to believe in it's beauty."

And she looked at me as if she expected me to say

something. So I told her about telling Allen I'm going to become a Buddhist. She said it hurt to laugh.

November 11

Happy Veteran's Day, Basil. Oh, I just remembered something our old preacher, Dr. Swofford, did right. When Basil was dying, he was deeply concerned about killing all those Chinese soldiers in Korea. He told Dr. Swofford he was sure God could not forgive a man for "mowing them down like grass." But Dr. Swofford said God loves us no matter what. I never in my all days heard a preacher talk so much about love. He told Basil that his salvation was secured by the blood of Jesus. He read from Paul's letter to the Romans, "Neither life nor death nor angels nor principalities nor things seen nor things unseen can separate us from the love of God which is in Christ Jesus." I believe old Basil got the point. You could learn something from the old timers, Arnold Chister, God bless you.

November 12

More angels, more rainbows, more waterfalls, more beautiful music. It energizes her. She sits up in bed and tells me and Mrs. Conley about it. Mrs. Conley said she has heard other people talk about it. They both sound crazy to me, but I found God to be like John Wayne and the Seventh Cavalry at the rim of the Grand Canyon, so I'm sure people would think me a tad loopy.

November 13

Allen played a couple of minutes. Dribbled, passed. I don't care. I love the game. These guys are so young, so strong. They move in their bodies without thinking about it. I hope they can remember these times fifty years from now. I played basketball in high school. I have always loved sports because of that and softball in the spring. And yes, now that I think about it, I remember running and jumping and shooting. Oh, Allen, look at the basket, baby. Take a shot.

November 14

John Prine has a song called, "The Oldest Baby In The World." Right now, that's Irene Butterworth. She coos when I bring her candy and baked pastries we call "sticky gooies." Maybe I'm making this up, but she seems to glow. I keep thinking every moment, every moment, every moment is precious, but I am so tired. S. J. and Charles are like married people. It's not healthy, but they are so much help at Irene's. They sweep, mop, do laundry and cook. I help them, but they've taken the lead at both houses. I run errands, watch her meds, pay her bills. Sometimes she is so gone into the next world, it's like she's looking back, asking me to come with her. I'd love to, baby, but the Yankees are looking real good for next season.

November 15

Basketball is so different from baseball. I don't understand women who turn their noses up at sports and act like the whole thing is just mass boredom. Within the confines of any basketball game is the whole drama of life. Well, that's a slight exaggeration, but think about it. Each team anticipates possibilities before the tip off, birth, dreams, a new day. Those possibilities get realized or slaughtered as each score rises or falls on the board. Like Shakespeare said, they're all out there playing parts, the super star, the team players, the big, slow white boys, the little fast white boys. Oh, I know I think too much about race, but race has changed sports forever. Anybody wanna argue with that? I'm praying Allen will break out. Look at the basket, baby. Shoot the ball.

November 16

Not much longer now. She has started to rattle. It is a sound that comes from the deep in her congested lungs. I asked Arnold about praying, "Thy will be done." He said it is a healing prayer. We didn't say anything for just a second or two. I asked him if he thought she could be healed. He asked me what I thought. I rolled my lips in and squeezed them and nodded.

I sit and look at her and fight sleep.

Her kids have come and gone. They're not much good. They have their own lives.

November 17

That's it. She left about four this morning. Why do people almost always do that? Maybe they need the world around them to be as quiet as possible before they can let go and flow away. Kelly White was there, passing her hands and sniffing, her face wet with tears. Eunice sang, "Alleluias," and I held up, pretending that a train was not driving through the center of my soul, ripping and tearing.

November 18

I stood in front of my closet looking at my clothes for 15 minutes this morning before I realized I was standing in front of my closet looking at my clothes. It took a long time to write that sentence. The house filled up with kin and covered dishes. Arnold moved among us like a janitor emptying ashtrays. He's been a rock. I let him hug me and pray for me when he first came over this morning.

November 19

Arnold preached a beautiful eulogy. Told things I'd never heard like how she'd worked for the defense department during Vietnam. Talked about her courage and the two fights she had fought with cancer. Her dutiful family did the right amount of eye-wiping and nose drying, but nobody has offered to remove this locomotive from my chest.

He read from Psalm 130: "If thou, Lord should mark iniquities, who could stand? But there is forgiveness with thee, that thou may be feared."

November 20

A crane. I need somebody to back a crane up and lift this locomotive off my chest. I locked myself out of the house. Bubba came and climbed in the window and got me in. I didn't think to ask him what he saw in Charlene.

November 21

I left the lights on in my car. Bubba came and jumped me off. He wouldn't let me pay him anything either time.

November 22

My doctor's a girl, too. God, they're everywhere. God, I mean that as a prayer. I know you are here. I know you love me. I am not being irreverent. She prescribed an anti-depressant. So I'm depressed now?

November 23

Allen wanted to talk. I felt terrible. You mean these children are still living with me? Maybe they've noticed that I hadn't noticed? I sure hope not. Allen was real serious. "Aunt Beverly, I got to tell you something." He's gotten some girl pregnant. That was my first thought. "The morning Aunt Irene died, she came and sat on the edge of my bed and talked to me." He had my undivided attention. "She told me good-bye, and told me to take care of you. She said I can hit a jumper from outside. She told me to look at the basket and shoot." I nodded, and spoke very quietly when I said, "Good advice." "But here's the really weird part. I had known the whole time that somebody was standing behind her, but I hadn't thought to look and see who it was. Then I did look. It was my mama." I asked him, "Did she say anything?" He said, "No, but when Aunt Irene said I could score from outside, she nodded her head." I nodded, too. "Look at the basket, baby. Take that shot."

November 24

Arnold asked me if the Hospice folks had brought by any books on grief. I said, "Yes." And the likelihood of my reading anything any time soon? About like the likelihood of the moon landing on my house.

November 25

Thump. Thump. Thump. He's coming home from practice and playing again in my driveway. I take this as a good sign.

November 26

Out of the blue, S. J. asked me, "Will I go to college?" I looked around the room. Out of my numbness, my dull pain, my broken heart, I asked her, "Who told you that you weren't going to college?" She said in the beautiful, flat North Carolina mountain accent, "Mama and Daddy didn't go." I thought about it for a minute and answered as best as I could, "Kids in foster care get a lot of help with the expenses of college, but the brain stuff you have to do pretty much on your own. You think you can handle it?" She studied me like I might be kidding with her or messing with her mind. "I can do anything I set my heart on." So, I asked her, "Is your heart set on going to college and doing well once you get there?" She nodded and said, "Oh yes, Aunt Beverly. Oh yes."

November 27

And I will die someday. You can bet cash money I've been thinking a lot about that here lately. I turn seventy-one next week, and I've heard people talk about three score and ten all my life. Three score and ten is in the Bible somewhere, and an awful lot of people die somewhere in that vicinity. The rest of us die later. I will rise in the arms of my savior, and he and his angels will take me into that land beyond the river they call the sweet forever. I will see my grandparents, my parents, Basil and his family, and I will see Irene Butterworth, freckle-faced and red-headed as she was as a young woman. I just know that's the truth. It will be a delightful party. I am looking there instead of into the aching cave which is my own heart at this moment.

November 28

Thump, thump, thump. In some future day, archeologists will wonder at the smoothness of my driveway in comparison to those of my neighbors. Maybe he is wearing smooth the jagged edges in his heart.

November 29

Sarah Jane asked me tonight what I'd think about her marrying Charles someday. I told her she's 14 years old. She said women years ago got married at 14. And pregnant, I thought but did not say. "What kind of young man do you think Charles is?" I asked her knowing full well both her answer and mine and feeling a tad surprised that I didn't really believe there would be much difference. She leaned into the door frame of the kitchen where I was going over some of my bills and making sure Irene's were getting paid. "He's the kindest, most gentle, most considerate human being on the face of the earth." I had to laugh, not hard, not making fun of her, though I was sorely tempted. She asked what was so funny, and I just shook my head. "Surely you'd be a fool not to marry a man like that," I said finally. I had to breathe through my nose not to laugh again really hard, really long, really loud.

November 30

Hard day. Everybody was cranky. I've been trying to help Irene's kids clean out her house. They'll sell it and that will be that. Their lives were cradled here, but they are long gone. I'm glad Wilson stayed here, at least. He and Charlene are doing well with preacher girl and marriage counseling. They're paying her! Imagine that. You mean to tell me Elizabeth and Arnold can't make it on two preacher salaries? Money is such an interesting piece of this puzzle we call life.

December 1

Candy canes and oranges. My Lord and my God, this will be our first Christmas together since I went out to the Grand Canyon and found you more real and more powerful and more alive than I ever imagined possible. These will be some very different Advent candles, a very different tree standing in the living room, more presents this year. The Department of Social Services will help me with gifts for Allen and Keith and S. J. So much to do, so much to plan, how wonderful!

December 2

Santa and reindeer, lights all over people's houses, trucks haul Christmas trees out of the mountains. I still move like I'm in Jello, grieving and crying and standing in front of my closets. It will take me months before I can pretend to be normal. But the kids are wonderful for keeping me grounded. Eunice and Charlene and yes, even Arnold, they all call to check on me, make sure I'm all right.

December 3

Joy to the World. Hark the Herald Angels Sing. Silent Night. The December calendar pulses with all that is going on, and there is so much. Some ballet company in Asheville is doing "The Nutcracker." Every church and half the houses in the county are putting stuff in their yards. Sometimes it feels totally disconnected. I think about this church in town that puts up these plywood wise men riding plywood camels. I wonder, "What does that have to do with the spirit of the living God?" Maybe it means something to the people with the plywood camels. But maybe not.

December 4

Thump. Boom. Thump thump. Boom. The booms come as the ball hits the backboard in my driveway. Allen comes home after every practice and practices some more. Keith gets out there with him. Dear God, sometimes a little brother is the greatest gift in the universe. Since Irene is gone, it's easier for me to get to games. Once the game is decided, either a big loss or a big win, Allen gets into the game. But he stands on the sidelines and cheers and cheers, and when he is on the court, he has more confidence. Is that the meaning of life? Confidence. He took a shot tonight. Missed. Came home. Thump. Thump. Boom.

December 5

Death is the cussedest thing. It's like an interrupted trip. When Wilson was little, Basil didn't want to take him to the amusement park at Myrtle Beach, so I got in the car and took him. It was pouring rain, and I skidded into the back of this idiot who was driving too slow, or maybe I was driving too fast. Pour old Wilson thought "that's that." You could tell from the look on his face, but the cop who investigated took us to the airport to rent a car, and I drove that rental car to the amusement park. We only rode one ride, but you could tell it made him happy. It was a whirly-gig ride and I got pretty sick, but if I hadn't taken him over there, it would have been a little death for him, a disappointment based on thinking life was gonna be one way and having it end up another way.

December 6

Arnold came over and sat with me. He's so goofy and crazy. You'd think God would ordain nothing but Charlton Heston and John Wayne types. He grinned and asked me how I am. "Lousy," I said with a deadpan intended to kill his grin. It worked. "I'm sorry," he said. Of course, he's sorry. That's all very sweet. But I'm the one this happened to. Her kids don't hurt like I hurt. Eunice doesn't hurt like I hurt. My foster kids don't hurt like I hurt, although maybe S. J. does really badly miss her Aunt Irene, but nobody really hurts the way I hurt. Nobody.

December 7

Pearl Harbor. Now, that was a hurting. Talk about an interrupted trip. We weren't even at war. Those sailors thought we might not get into the war, and then they died. Nobody who lived through that war will forget it — the way people pulled together, the way we helped each other, the way people turned to God. The churches were full. We don't need another war, but we could sure use something to make us that caring, that courageous again.

December 8

Doris Betts came to town tonight, spoke at the community college. Eunice talked me into going. We took Charles and S. J. My little princess wanted to argue a little. I pointed at the car. She got in it. Doris Betts is some kind of writer from Chapel Hill. She talked about books and writing and told some funny stories. We laughed and enjoyed her energy. She is very high energy. Somehow Eunice ended up dragging us to a reception after her talk, and we all ended up sitting on a couch and on chairs around her. And as amazing as it may seem, she spent the whole time asking us about ourselves. This famous writer lady was interested in us?

December 9

Oh, Come All Ye Faithful. Oh, Little Town of Bethlehem. Oh, oh, oh, oh, I miss Irene so. The days go by okay, but sometimes I bury my face in a pillow and sob like the sobbing itself will either kill me or cure me. Sometimes it feels like I have the choice, die or get better. Then I remember I do have that choice. Oh, God, you who talked to Abraham about counting stars, send me new stars to count. Amen.

December 10

Wilson came by tonight after the ball game. Allen shot again. Missed again. As Wilson sat around the kitchen table with me, Allen thumped and boomed in the driveway, Keith out there with him. S. J. and Charles "doing homework," as they put it, in front of the television. Wilson started off by observing, "There's a lot going on around here, huh?" I nodded. Get to it, boy. You've got something you want to tell me. He said he's discovered in his counseling with preacher girl that he has issues from his childhood, that his daddy and I never seemed to be satisfied with him, that he was never good enough. I wrapped the fingers on my left hand with the fingers on my right hand. I drew a long breath, bit my bottom lip, sniffed, and said, "That's right, Wilson, you never were good enough, but neither was anybody else. Maybe it was because your daddy couldn't ever seem to make enough money or maybe it was because I couldn't ever seem to make enough love, but for some reason we twisted an ankle early on and limped through the whole marriage. I'm sorry, son. I'm just as sorry as I can be, but last May, when I made my first trip to the canyon, I found the Lord in ways I didn't think were possible. I cried like a baby while he washed over me like a waterfall. I'm still a cranky old lady, but I'm working as hard as I can to forgive everybody who ever hurt me and wash out all the hurt in my life. The biggest forgiveness work I have to do is to forgive myself. I know Elizabeth Chister is talking to the two of you about forgiveness, so I won't go on and on. Just do it, Wilson. Do it and do it and do it some more." We talked two more hours.

December 11

I called Elizabeth on the phone and told her I was sorry for every bad thought I ever had about her. She laughed and I asked her what was so cussed funny? She said, "Well, Beverly Roberts you are so kind to call and offer an apology, but if the truth were known, I can't say that all my thoughts of you have been entirely kind." We both got a good laugh out of that.

December 12

I took everybody but Allen to the Burger Barn. He was still at ball practice. Charles ended up in front with me. When I noticed S. J. and Keith were chatting in the back, I leaned over to him and asked him, "You hate my guts, don't you?" "No, ma'am, Miss Beverly, you give me and Sarah Jane lots of freedom, but not enough to get into trouble. I like that." Bless his heart. He may be lying, but it was a sweet lie.

December 13

Arnold tells us there is a pregnant teenager on her way to Bethlehem to have a baby, that he will be the savior of the world. It seems to me that baby has done a beautiful job of saving the dead. I know Basil found him walking that lonesome valley at the end. Irene looked into a world full of waterfalls and rainbows. And maybe Wilson and Charlene are finding him in dealing with their childhood pain, learning to forgive cranky old women like me who are never satisfied with anything. But saving the world? Oh, sweet Jesus, try a little harder. Oh come, oh come, Emmanuel, and ransom captive Israel.

December 14

My 71st birthday. They did a great job. Allen even arranged for Eunice to pick him up from practice early. Cake, ice cream, the works. Wilson and Charlene, their kids, Arnold and Elizabeth, their kids, my kids. I hugged them all better than I have ever hugged anybody, especially Elizabeth Chister. If she can save Wilson and Charlene's marriage, I don't care how much I have to face what a mean old woman I am. Happy Birthday, you mean old Beverly, you.

December 15

Keith has worked his way into five hundred dollars. He's bagging groceries in town, arranging his own rides after school. I have no doubt that a motorcycle of some ilk will be sitting in my driveway on Christmas morning. He'll put a big red bow on it and tell me it's my Christmas present since I won't have to drive him so much. People will call me crazy for letting it happen, but it has saved this boy's life. It and the Lord, of course.

December 16

S. J. and Charles have presented me with excellent report cards. I've talked to the guidance department. They say it's too soon to start talking about college, but I got some addresses and have ordered materials from nearby schools. We'll paper the wall in S. J.'s room.

December 17

With all three kids in school, I have more time to myself. I walk. I clean house. I go to meetings with Eunice. All that praying and emptying out is sure a load of work. Sometimes I worry that some of us are just going through the motions of forgiving, not really letting it go, not really letting God wash us all like waterfalls, but then I remember that I was in such awful shape when all this started and I feel like I'm in such a better place now. Maybe sometimes we have to go through the motions of opening ourselves to

God so that when he does show up we'll be in shape to do the heavy lifting.

December 18

Dana, Charles's mama, is going to some of the meetings with us. She has become my team member. We share a meal about every two weeks now, maybe not that much, but we aim for that. We sit together at ball games sometimes. I asked one time after a meeting who she has to forgive. Don't ask me why I asked, because I almost never ask. She laughed long and high, "A lot of white people, girl. A lot of white people."

December 19

Arnold preached on God establishing righteousness, called it, "setting things right." Reminded us that many of the Jesus prophecies were about bringing low the mighty and building up the weak. The trick there is to know which is which; and for me, anyway, the trick is to always be building up the weak.

December 20

Last school day before they get out for the holidays. Holiday tournament. We played East Burke. Darcas Williams got hurt late in the third quarter. Allen went into a close game. Confidence. Eyes set like an eagle. I prayed like my house was on fire. One minute into the fourth quarter he was open on the left side. Took the pass. Looked at the basket. Swish. Three points! All the angels in glory sang, "Alleluia!" He played a good game the rest of the night, scored once more on a short jumper, rebounded well, got a foul shot. When the game was over I hugged him so hard I couldn't tell my tears from his sweat.

December 21

And yes, it's a fairy tale, but who knows? Maybe life's a cussed fairy tale! Frank reached through the little hole at the bottom of the mesh screen in the prison visitor room, squeezed his oldest boy's hand, and twanged in that sweet mountain accent of his, "You done good, Allen. I'm real proud of you, fella. I sure enough am." We laughed and cried and gave Frank the new socks and underwear we'd brought him for Christmas. They won't let you give prisoners much. He was real sweet to S. J. and Keith, too. He doesn't know about Charles. In time. In time.

December 22

As we left the prison, Frank had passed me a note that said, "I owe you." I wrote him back and mailed it today. "No, you owe them, and you'll do fine. You'll make the phone calls when you can and sometimes even write them (I've enclosed stamps), and you'll be the best daddy you know how to be. It's only seven years, Frank, and after that, there will be weddings and grandchildren and lots of times for you to tell them how proud you are. They love to hear that from you, Frank. They want to hear it and hear it and hear it. I don't know when you tell them you're sorry about their mama, but I know they know it, and I know you'll know the right time to tell them."

December 23

I'd love to bring the whole world to the rim of my Grand Canyon, but I can't do it. I hear preachers say in revival meetings, "It's the simplest thing in the world," and I reckon at times it is. But it is also very, very complicated. God is just starting out with Allen and S. J. and Charles and Keith (the motorcycle arrived this morning.) God is moving heaven and earth with some ministries in some places, feeding the hungry and dealing with prisoners and stuff like that. And with me and Eunice and the rest of the old people in the world? Well, he's doing all kinds of things, working us and playing with us and ordering our lives for the day when we get our rainbows and waterfalls. Miracles are always everywhere. Oh, God, I am so grateful. Thank you, for life.

December 24

S. J. played Mary in the Nativity. The irony is not lost on me. Hopefully Jesus will be the only baby she gives birth to for at least ten or twelve years. Angels picking their noses and shepherds in bathrobes were absolutely beautiful. Arnold ran around like a chicken with his head cut off. But for some reason it didn't bother me near as much this year. The church was nearly packed. Wilson and Charlene were there with their kids. Wilson's AA sponsor, Max, sat with them. My friend Dana brought her kids. Eunice sat with a bunch of the folks from the forgiveness meetings. The Rev. Elizabeth Chister even brought a delegation from the Methodist Church. I know they were shocked to hear we read from the same Bible. Just kidding. We sang, "Silent night. Holy night. All is calm. All is bright." And it was.

I still don't like his haircut.

365 Ways to Criticize · the · Preacher

Pat Jobe